The Nerd and the Neighbor
Oak Creek Book 1
By Lainey Davis

The Nerd and the Neighbor

Oak Creek Book 1

By Lainey Davis

Join my newsletter and never miss a new release!

© 2019 Lainey Davis

Many thanks to Nicky Lewis and Keith G for editorial input.

1

Hunter

I should feel excited today. I know this. I'll be going back home, where I can piss with ease and eat food that tastes and feels like food. Hell, I can sleep without being tethered to the wall. But all I can focus on is my unfinished work. I'm so close to finding answers. If I had another 6 months I think I could change everything…but I failed to find the answers in the time allotted.

I only get six months up here. I have to just trust the science and believe whoever they're sending to replace me will do the work. Trust is not my strong suit. Neither is handing off my work to another scientist.

Digger floats by as I'm packing up my belongings. I don't have much. Just some plant samples I want to bring back in the capsule. He asks, "What are you gonna eat first, Crawdad?"

"You know I hate being called that," I tell him, ignoring the question. I definitely will not miss being forced into repeated social interactions with this same group of people. At least everyone up here has a firm grasp of the scientific method and an interest in math. Digger—everyone has a stupid nickname, too—glares at me, though, so I appease him. He's got three months remaining, after all.

"Strawberries," I tell him. "Maybe a pineapple, if they can find one." Digger's mouth waters as he helps me and one of the Russian scientists get situated inside the capsule that will take us home. The two of us will be crammed in there for hours until we touch down on the ground. The actual ground! It's funny. Our float back to Earth will take less time than my eventual plane ride back to Texas. A little over three hours to drift from the International Space Station back to the life I'm supposed to feel excited to re-embrace.

The truth is, I have no idea where the Space Agency will send me next. My research, at this point, belongs to them, and so I belong to them. The thought makes me uneasy, but who else has the right resources to support tissue research in a zero-gravity environment?

The Russian and I are silent as we plummet downward, anticipating the first impact. I've done this before. I don't think he has, though. My siblings would probably talk to him and offer comfort. I can't bring myself to do it. I'm waiting for the hit.

The first parachute opens and it's like a car crash. I feel my bones shake in their sockets, and I embrace it because it's the first time I've sensed gravity in half a year. Each time, I forget. I forget what it's like to feel the weight of my frame, to feel my blood moving inside my veins.

The soft landing jets ignite just before we crash into the steppe of Kazakstan. Only then does it occur to me that I haven't heard from my wife. My mother emailed repeatedly, wanting up-to-the-minute information. My wife should have reached out, right? Should I have contacted her? We only get to use the satellite phone once a week, but we have unlimited access to our email. All my brothers and my sister sent good luck messages, and all of them made some dumb joke about how I don't believe in luck. Heather should have at least emailed. The realization that I can't remember the last time I communicated with my wife washes over me like an uncomfortable haze. I can feel the weight of that, too.

This is my second mission since we were married. That would take a toll on any marriage. All the separation. She's likely having a difficult time. I should miss her, probably. The way I miss fresh fruit and sunshine. Don't people miss their spouse when they're separated?

The capsule skids to a halt and someone opens the lid. Smells wash over me. I forgot that, too. I haven't smelled anything or felt the earth beneath me. Haven't felt heat like this. Seen daylight bathing the earth. We're immobile in our landing suits, so we have to be extracted from the capsule like babies being pulled from a car seat. I tolerate this because I know as soon as they set me down, they're going to hand me a plate of fruit and the satellite phone.

My mother tried to pull strings to be here at the landing site, but the best she could do was book a room in the village nearby. Very few people say no to Rose Mitchell, and I can envision the argument with the director of the space program. I try to laugh out loud at that image, but my mouth feels like it's stuffed with cotton. I realize I'm parched.

The thirst is immense and I can feel my lips cracking in the sun while I wait for someone to unfasten my suit and let me use my hands again. I'm aware of the media, cameras in my face, reporters firing questions at me and the Russian guy. I start to panic, actually, even though I know this isn't rational. I know all my bodily systems are being monitored. Nobody would let anything happen to me. My mind seems disconnected from my central nervous system, though, and the panicked thoughts begin to rush over me. I think again about Heather, wondering why she wouldn't reach out when her husband was floating through the universe in a damn tin can.

I'm on the verge of blackness when I'm handed the phone. I see myself reach out to accept it, as if from far away, and I bring the phone to my ear. I hear it ring. Again. Again. Then my wife's voice comes over the voicemail. *This is strange,* I think, as I drift out of consciousness. *She should answer.*

When I open my eyes, I'm surrounded by bright, white light, and then I see the form of my mother. My senses seem to re-engage one at a time. I smell disinfectant and saline fluid, a slight tinge of bleach. I take stock of my body and realize I'm lying down in a bed, hospital sheets scratching my bare skin. The light weight of the sheets against my limbs...I smile as I notice the feeling of it all. Then comes my sense of hearing, and Rose Mitchell is giving someone a lecture. "How you could allow my son to become dehydrated is well beyond me," she snarls. "You haven't figured out a better methodology for transporting these heroes back to Earth? They're up there for months doing research in the name of our nation and you drop them like an egg in a shoe box. Plop! Back to the ground. No water. You should be ashamed."

"Ma," I croak. It's good to see her. I don't make it home to Oak Creek often, even when I'm on this planet.

"Oh *there* you are, Hunter. Sweetheart, shouldn't you be advising your colleagues about dehydration? You have heat stroke, Hunter Crawford. How on *earth* does someone contract heat stroke when they're being so closely monitored? When did you last have a drink of water?"

I gesture toward the IV in my arm. "Ma," I try again. "Where's Heather?"

She sighs. "Oh, sweetheart."

I really am the only one to blame for this. I know that. I don't communicate well. This has always been a challenge for me—expressing my feelings. Thinking about Heather's feelings. When she's not yelling at me, she's often explaining that I don't value her. Which isn't true, but I understand that what she means is I do not make *her* feel that she's a priority for me.

I look around our empty condo. She took everything except my equipment and my clothes. All the furniture. The toothpaste. She left a note taped to my microscope telling me her lawyer would reach out with paperwork. I assess the moments leading up to my arrival back in Houston. The media is camped outside my building, frothing at the mouth to get the scoop on the scorned astronaut.

I can ignore them with ease. I just walk past them. That first day home, alone, I opened the door and my primary concern was for my frozen plant samples, followed by concern for my microscope. I really didn't feel very strongly about the absence of my wife.

Heather is right. She is not a priority to me. She was…comfortable. Marrying her made sense. Or it did at the time.

Had I ever made real space for her? We met when I was in graduate school the first time. Heather dictated all the terms of our relationship, told me when to show up for dinner, how to dress for the occasion. I thrived under that treatment. No fuss. No work for me to do outside my research. Once we moved in together, she did the shopping and planned our free time together. I liked that, too. She made things very simple for me. I see it now.

I hear my phone ring and stoop to pick it up from the hardwood floor. "This is Hunter Crawford."

The low, rumbling voice of my supervisor comes through the line, inquiring about my health, making the type of small talk we both detest. I'm seconds away from curtly asking him what he wants, when he sighs and says, "Crawford, they cut your funding."

"Excuse me?"

"The agency no longer wants to prioritize the study of microgravity on human tissues."

"Burt, that's irresponsible. What the hell are you talking about?"

I hear him telling me there's no further funding for studying the ways human bodies change during space flight. I know he's talking about administration cuts, and I'm aware of him suggesting I might find a position in academia. Academia! We both know I'm not meant to teach.

But as he's talking, I don't think. I climb into my car and drive to the research lab even as I'm hanging up with Burt. As if I'm watching a movie, I see myself kick open the door to the building and stomp past the receptionist.

I watch myself pound my fist on the director's door and I note the concerned look in his eyes as I barge in and demand that he reinstate my program. This work I do is vital to the future of the space program. "You have all insisted that space exploration is the key to the survival of our species, Alan!"

There's an edge to my voice I'm not familiar with. I can tell I sound unstable. This is unlike me. "How can you send astronauts past the stratosphere without researching what it will do to their bodies??"

"Hunter, I'd hoped you and Burt could discuss this calmly. I know you're newly back and you're still a little jet-lagged."

"Jet lag? Are you fucking kidding me? You're closing my research program! What about the fucking tissue samples I left in the Space Station? This is decades of my life, Alan! I want my work."

I don't register what he says to me next. I think about my empty apartment, my absent wife. I think about the carefully arranged notes I left by the slides, the tissue chips I built to mimic the functions of various organs. All I have ever wanted is to understand the way cells function, to unlock the secrets of life.

Of all life.

Like a fiend, I have pursued this research since I was a teenager, begging to assist in the labs at the college where my mother now serves as president.

Alan places a hand on my shoulder and tries to nudge me toward the door. I look down at his hand on my body, and I watch myself grab his arm, twisting and clenching. I see the fear in his eyes as I squeeze his bones together. My life flashes before me until I'm a kid again, wrestling with my brothers by the creek.

I was always smaller, even if I was the oldest, so I had to understand physics and leverage. Like a frantic child, I snarl as I wrench Alan's arm from my shoulder and shove him away from me until he stumbles into the wall.

Panting, my chest heaving, I look up to see security officers shouting into their radios as they flock in to haul me off the property.

2

Abigail

As I pull into my driveway, I realize I'm dreading going inside. *That's not good,* I think. Things have definitely been...stagnant. I sigh and look down at my polo and khakis. Working at my dad's construction firm was never part of my plan. Not that I had a plan exactly, but Baker and Sons just isn't a destination for me. This was supposed to be a part-time job while I finished school.

I look at Jack's truck in the driveway. I can tell he hasn't moved it from yesterday, which means he's been home the whole time. Again. Layoffs happen to everyone. He's taken it so personally, retreating deeper and deeper inside himself the longer he goes without work.

As I go through the mental checklist of "get a job" items I think he should do, I realize Jack is most of the reason I'm biting my lip right now, lingering in the driveway. Things just haven't been good. He wasn't supposed to be a destination, either, I remind myself.

Jack was someone I dated in school. Then I just never got around to breaking up with him, I guess. I moved into the house he bought, and gradually took on more of the roles he thought I should, and more of myself slipped away each passing month.

I exhale and grab my lunch bag, steeling myself to go inside. The hinges on the side door squeak as I nudge it open with my hip, juggling my lunch bag and the mail. "Hey, Babe," I call out. The air smells stale in here. Jack grunts from the couch. He's watching one of those judge shows on tv, and starts berating the defendant. "Babe, I don't want to hear about those people's bad choices, if that's ok, it's been a long—"

"Well *excuse* me," he sneers. "So sorry if my 'low brow' entertainment offends you." He throws an empty soda can across the room. I cringe, thinking about the splatters of sticky liquid that will surely dribble onto the carpet. We're going to get ants.

He stomps past me into the bedroom and slams the door. I sigh and stoop to clean up the soda, absent-mindedly scrubbing the rug.

This would actually be a great scene, I think. Late at night, once Jack is asleep— passed out if I'm honest—I've been trying something new. Something I always wanted to do. I started writing a novel.

I get a thrill just thinking about it, saved inside my laptop in a locked folder.

I know I shouldn't feel the need to password protect something on my own laptop in the house where I'm supposed to live as an equal. But things with Jack have been so strained. He's not the same person he was three months ago. He was fine as a boyfriend. Attentive, kind, generous. I think getting laid off triggered a depression in him, shook his sense of himself as a man.

And I'm just not ready to share this fiction whim with him yet.

I've been carrying the mortgage, but I don't mind. He wasn't asking me for any rent or anything before. I've been living here basically free for a year. Sure, I chipped in for groceries when he lets me whip my card out first, but I think Jack liked supporting me. I glance toward the bedroom, where I hear him moving around, making noises. Angry.

My stomach growls, and I feel a sense of sadness that I turned down a dinner invite with my family. Again. One of these days, I ought to just go over there without Jack and enjoy myself. Lately, he's said no to my dad's "charity" every time they invite us over for supper, like they've done once a week since I moved out. I see my dad and brothers every day at the office, but I haven't seen my mother in weeks. I miss talking to her in person.

I fire off a quick text to her, saying I am sorry again for missing tonight. *Jack is feeling really down,* I write, wondering if she can read between the lines. Probably not. My mom seems pretty set in her belief that I need to settle down with a "good man who can take care of us."

As I slide the phone back in my pocket, I shriek because the bedroom door flies open abruptly.

"Abby! What the fuck is this?" Jack has my laptop in one hand. His eyes are wild, angry.

"You scared me," I tell him, bringing my hand to my chest. I'm still squatting on the carpet where I'd been cleaning up the spilled soda. I start to rise to my feet, but Jack stomps over to me.

I actually feel afraid, and I don't like it. This isn't ok.

I shouldn't feel afraid in my house, of the man who is supposed to love me.

"You have locked files on here? What? Are you keeping shit from me? In my own house?" Small flecks of spit fly from his mouth as he screams in my face, and I know that I have to leave this house.

Immediately.

I scan the room, noting my keys on the peg by the side door. But Jack is standing in my face, his chest heaving.

"You need to calm down, Jack. This isn't ok."

"Calm down? Fuck you, Abigail! Calm down?" And then he shoves me backwards—places a hand on my shoulder and pushes with all the strength of his six-foot frame. I stumble back a few steps before catching my balance.

I'm so startled that he touched me in anger that I can't think of what to say or do. I bite my lower lip and try to walk past him, toward my keys. I yelp as a searing pain rips through my head. Jack has hold of my ear, painfully twisting my head and pulling me across the room to the couch.

"Unlock it," he whisper-yells, still holding my ear. "Open the folder. I want to see what you're fucking typing about me in there."

"Jack, you're hurting me!"

"Open the mother fucking folder!"

I start to cry as he tugs my head over toward the laptop now propped on his knee. I can't explain why I don't just do as he says and show him the contents of the folder, but for some reason I just do not want him to see my novel. It feels private. Sacred.

My secret is mine. Whatever the cost.

Jack snarls again and releases my ear, shoving me back against the couch. He meets my eye, and I see that any resemblance to the pleasant young man I met is gone.

All that remains is clouded in anger.

Hot fury twists his face until I barely recognize him. Jack cracks the laptop screen backwards over his knee, the metal grinding and splintering. I scream as the screen shatters. He throws the useless computer across the room.

A sense of calm washes over me then, as I rise from the couch. Wordlessly, I stoop to pick up my broken laptop. Without a glance back, I walk toward the door, snag my keys, and start to drive.

A few minutes later, the adrenaline leaves me and I notice my head is throbbing. I assess my ear at a stoplight. I don't think I need medical care. Just some ice and sleep somewhere safe. I consider driving to my parents' house, but the thought of explaining all this feels like too much. I just keep driving.

Soon, I cross from Ohio into Pennsylvania, and I pull off the highway near Pittsburgh. One of the chain hotels boasts free dinner on Tuesdays, and a hot tub, which both sound perfect until I realize I'll have to sit in public with my swollen ear and I didn't pack any clothes, let alone a bathing suit.

I chew my lip again and look around the parking lot, spotting a drive through fast food chain. Five minutes later, I'm checked into a room with a bag of greasy fries and a milk shake. I press a baggie of ice against my head with one hand and dial my father's office phone.

I don't want to disappear without a trace, but I also can't stand the thought of talking to my family tonight. Dad's voicemail message begins, his singsong voice announcing "Baker and Sons Construction—finest work in Greenwood. Leave a message and one of the Bakers will call you back. You have my word about that!"

"Dad, it's Abby," I say, my voice wavering more than I intended. "I'm sorry for the short notice, but I won't be in the office tomorrow. Or the rest of this week, actually. I need to get away for awhile. Nothing's wrong. I don't want you and Mom to worry." I sigh. Of course they'll worry. "I just needed a change of scenery. Sorry again."

A few minutes later, I toss my empty cup in the trash by my bed and snap off the light. I drift off into a dreamless, exhausted sleep, not knowing what the future holds.

3

Hunter

I stare out the window of my brother Archer's truck, watching the scenery blur past. My car, along with the meager pile of my other possessions, is in a shipping container en route to Oak Creek. Part of the discharge package from the Space Agency.

That's what they're calling it, anyway. Despite news of my breakdown leaking all over the place, the official word is that I resigned after my mission.

They didn't even have the balls to go public with the information that the research program is being canceled. I assessed the financials, and I still don't have enough to move forward with my tissue research on my own, not even with my severance.

And so, with no wife, no furniture, and no prospects, I am headed home to Oak Creek. I know I've been the main focus of the gossip mill there, but I never can find it in me to care about those things. Heather indicated my aloofness was part of the problem. I don't care enough about anything when it comes to other people, apparently.

I didn't call my brother to come fetch me. I'm pretty sure my mother sent him. He showed up as the movers were packing my lab equipment and told me to get in the truck, and so here I am.

We cross into Kentucky and Archer starts singing along with the country music on the radio.

"I hate this type of music," I state without looking at him.

"Tough shit, Hunter," Archer says during an instrumental lick. "You find a place to stay yet?"

I shake my head. I thought I'd stay at our parents' house, which seems a fitting place for a man whose wife left and career exploded.

Archer taps out the rhythm on the steering wheel and says, "I know you haven't been home in awhile. Dad turned each of our rooms into a different sort of theme. That's what he calls it. They bring in international students to stay in, like, The Meadow Room and The Obersvatory Room. It's like fucking Clue with kids from Thailand and Saudi Arabia sitting down for tea with Dad."

I grunt noncommittally. He grins. "Wanna crash at my place?"

I shrug. "I can buy someplace as soon as that can be arranged." At the next rest stop, Archer pulls out his phone and makes a call while I'm ordering our lunch. He tells me he found out about a duplex for sale right in town and will get me set up with a realtor. My kid brother is the only accountant in Oak Creek. He knows everyone, knows their business, and manages to remember every single birthday of every Oak Creek resident.

Mom likes to joke that he got all my social skills that I left behind in her womb. I can barely manage to figure out when people are joking.

Today I feel even less like working on it, and Archer shakes his head as I reserve our hotel room using single syllables.

It feels good to drive a car on the vast expanse of highway after spending so long cooped up in a tube with no gravity. Even if I hate the lack of fuel economy in my brother's beast of a truck, I appreciate the feel of my body in the deep leather seats. He props his feet on the dash while I take my turn, navigating toward eastern Pennsylvania on instinct. Archer looks at me for a long time before saying, "Jesus, Hunter. I've been waiting for you to say something."

I shrug without taking my eyes off the road. "Should have let me know, then. What were you hoping I'd say?"

"I don't know, man. Small talk! Fuck, dude, what must it have been like for those other space nerds to be up there with you for six whole months."

"It was fruitful in terms of research outcomes," I say, then I grit my teeth. "Though not as fruitful as I would have liked."

He laughs at me. "You going to take Ma up on the job offer?"

I see the exit for our next highway and put on my turn signal, ignoring my brother. Teaching undergraduate biology at Oak Creek College sounds less attractive than bankruptcy. Even if my mother calls me a Distinguished Guest Professor, it still feels very much like what it is: a charity offer for a man who has been blackballed throughout the bioresearch community.

Archer continues to stare at me, and I figure out that he's still waiting for a response.

"I told her I'd try for a semester," I say, accelerating onto four-lane road toward home. "Just until I finish a proposal for investors."

4

Abigail

In the morning, the side of my head still throbs, and a wave of emotion threatens to keep me in the uncomfortable, unfamiliar bed. I feel a rush of guilt at leaving my father and co-workers while I figure out whatever the hell it is I'm doing. I feel anger at Jack for betraying my trust. Most of all, I feel anger at myself for staying with him long enough for things to get so bad.

I should have noticed things weren't ok when he stopped wanting me to go see my parents. As my body and mind wake fully, a thousand memories rush through my mind until my entire relationship feels like a series of mistakes I made. I don't even know how to see what's healthy, apparently, until things get dangerous.

I decide to go to the free breakfast downstairs, and I pass a Business Center where nobody is using the ancient desktop computer or printer. While I wait for my waffle batter to cook in the griddle, I weigh my options. If I head back to Greenwood, I could maybe stay with my parents, but I'd have to tell them everything. Then they'd want to know why this is the first they're hearing about Jack sinking deeper into depression the longer he was unemployed.

Unless I went back right now, they might not even believe me that he laid his hands on me last night. He always put on such a big show of trying to impress my dad.

If they did believe me, I can also imagine my parents scolding me for staying with a loser who was out of work for so long. I sigh. My father viewed Jack as another son, since the moment I first brought him home. As soon as I started dating an HVAC guy, my contractor dad stopped asking me about school. They all stopped asking about my studies. Everything became about my boyfriend and whether he was doing well.

I had great grades in high school and kept a 4.0 all through community college. My parents didn't even know I managed to get a minor in professional communication as I completed my degree in business at a branch campus of the state university.

Slathering my waffle with as much syrup as I'd like, nobody to tell me I'm being wasteful, I try to remember what made me say yes to the quiet man finishing his HVAC certification in the same building as I took my first creative writing class.

I think, at the time, I was flattered to be noticed. Jack came up to me in the commons, where I was engrossed in my writing. He said I looked beautiful then, inspired. By the time I noticed that my family liked Jack more than I did, we were already planning to move in together.

That first semester when we got together, we'd go for long walks, and I'd talk to Jack about what I was writing. He didn't tell me that was the stuff of dreams and nonsense like my pragmatic parents did. Jack listened to my stories, said he'd like to read a book like that. He kissed me and asked me to tell him all my grand ideas.

And then eventually, he stopped asking.

After I eat, I look over at the business center again. I think about the smashed laptop in the trunk of my car, and walk over to the computer. I pull up the web browser and type WRITING JOBS. I scroll through a few pages of sales jobs. I scroll right on past a few newspaper positions I don't even feel qualified to apply for. But then I see something interesting.

SPEECH WRITER AND COMMUNICATOR NEEDED!
Busy college president needs a writer ASAP to help prepare speeches, remarks, correspondence. The college is exploring new partnerships. Candidate should begin immediately. Send samples and cover letter to Oak Creek College.

There's no name listed with the posting, no contact information. *They really* do *need help with communication,* I think. Oak Creek College. I think I've heard of that before—a small liberal arts school in Eastern PA. I search for it online and am charmed by the photographs. Long walkways lined with trees, old brick buildings. The town looks cute, too. I see a bunch of ads for little festivals and shops that sell everything from baked goods to tarot cards.

I chew on my bottom lip, feeling guilty. Could I walk away from my job at my dad's office? It's a good job, after all. I earn a nice wage, and he offers benefits.

But I never left Greenwood much. Not for college. Surely there are other "good jobs" out there in the world that feel more like…me.

I search the Oak Creek College website for the directory and see a phone number for the president's office. I only hesitate a moment before typing the number into my cell, and am startled when a very loud voice answers, "Hello! This is Rose!"

"Um…hi. I was calling about the writing job I saw—"

"When can you get here? Do you have experience?"

Woah. Okay. "Well, I have a minor in professional communication from the University of Ohio at—"

"That'll do. Just come in. Can you be here today? We're meeting with the computer engineers tomorrow."

I look at the time. It's around 8am and Oak Creek is five hours' drive from here. "It will take me until 1:30 to clear my schedule," I say.

I hear the woman sigh. "Fine. What's your name again? My secretary is out today. Tell the desk you're here to write remarks for Rose." By the time I open my mouth to say thank you for the opportunity, she's hung up the phone.

What a strange person…unless…I look around, thinking maybe someone is playing a prank. There is, of course, nobody nearby. I stand up, realizing I have nothing with me. Nothing to pack. Nothing to prepare. Nothing to wear other than these day-old khakis and my work polo from my father's company. Talk about starting out fresh. I wince as my ear throbs when I try to tuck my hair behind my ear.

I check out of the hotel and ask where the closest clothing store is that would be open this early. I hit the highway within the hour, wearing a respectable-if-cheap suit, feeling excitement in my belly rather than dread.

5

Hunter

I'll never know how Ed Hastings found out I was coming home. I'm sure my brother wouldn't tell the small-town rag editor on purpose, but the old coot probably was eavesdropping outside Arch's office when he said he was coming to pick me up.

At any rate, the ancient editor of the *Oak Creek Gazette* is waiting when we roll up to my parents' house that night. "Ed Hastings, *Oak Creek Gazette*," he says, shoving a recorder in my face as if I haven't known him since I was born. "Care to answer a few questions about your alleged fall from grace?"

"Now's not the time, Ed," my brother tells him, resting a hand on the old man's shoulder. I just grunt and walk toward my parents' house.

Undeterred, Ed shouts, "Our readers are going to want answers! Will Space Agency officials be coming to town for any alleged legal proceedings? What about your reported alimony payments to the estranged Mrs. Crawford?"

My father emerges from the house and the smile melts off his face at the sight of the reporter badgering me. "Ed, enough!" Dad doesn't shout often. The sound of him raising his voice is as unusual to me as it is effective for Ed, who backs down the walk and disappears around the corner. Dad turns to me, a smile lighting his eyes. "Good to have you back, son."

He shuffles us inside, where the aroma of his cooking wafts over me. It's been ages since I've eaten something fresh and home cooked. All our meals in the space station were calibrated, dehydrated, and tasteless, and I haven't been able to prepare anything since I got back. "Heather took all the cookware," I tell him, a non sequitur that doesn't faze him.

"Your mother told me all about it," he says, handing me a chunk of cheese. I don't typically like to eat dairy. Human bodies aren't meant to digest the milk of other mammals. My research into lactose intolerance confirms this. But the sharp cheddar hits my tastebuds and I know whatever negative reaction I'll experience is worth the cost of this.

I relax into a stool at the counter while Archer tells Dad about his latest video chat with our brother Fletcher. Fletch decided to hang out in France for awhile after filming the Tour de France. "He and Ma met up for some sort of wine tour," Archer gushes. Nobody expects me to say much, so I don't, settling into the platter of olives

13

and cheeses. My sister Diana arrives and kisses my cheek.

Her physical affection catches me off guard, and I stiffen at her touch. I don't particularly enjoy being touched, but I tolerate it from my family. Assessing my response to physical contact is on my list of research goals for someday.

"Hunter! Dude, I'm talking to you." Diana throws an olive at me.

"Sorry. I was…I wasn't paying attention."

"We can tell," she says, slugging down a gulp of white wine. "Anyway I was saying I'd love to get your input on my plant samples. When you get a chance."

Diana runs the Houseplant Haven here in Oak Creek. Her back office is a greenhouse where she's made it clear she conducts horticulture research, but won't tell us the details of her experiments. I raise a brow at her, curious about this sudden invitation into her lair. "You want me to see what you're working on?"

She shakes her head. "Nice try, bro. You're not going into my lab. But I want to show you one plant. I have a theory about light and soil composition, and I think I read your colleague was studying something similar in the space station."

Dad and Archer groan as Diana and I begin to discuss biology. My sister also has a PhD in biology, from Princeton, but never entered academia. She returned to Oak Creek soon after graduate school and opened the tiny shop, watering people's philodendrons when they go on vacation and keeping her actual source of income a mystery from the rest of us.

Archer sets the table and tries to steer the conversation away from our research. "I was telling Hunter there's no room here at the house because you and Ma are taking in stragglers," he says as he folds napkins and places the white china plates. I try and fail to remember the last time I ate food from a real plate with real silverware.

"I don't mind," I say, "although I'm hopeful the movers can park my storage pod here until I'm able to purchase the property Archer identified for me."

Just then, my mother bursts in the door. She brings with her a flurry of energy, always a whirlwind. "I'm home, my darlings," she says, kissing everyone once, but pulling me into her tiny body and squeezing me like a tube of toothpaste. "Mmmm, Hunter, I'm so excited you're coming in to work with me!"

"I don't know yet, Ma."

She waves her hand and tosses her suit jacket on the stool. "Nonsense. You're coming in with me tomorrow. I'm meeting with potential investors."

Diana and I stare at one another. I blink a few times and try to gather my thoughts about this announcement. "Since when does Oak Creek attract big-name corporate partners?"

Ma launches into an overview of her outreach this past year while I've been in space. She's really been drawing a lot of philanthropy into the college, and attracting students who go on to earn prestigious fellowships. One of her recent grads won a Pulitzer Prize and another earned a Field Medal. I start allowing myself to think a stint teaching with my mother won't be so pitiful after all. Ma has that affect on people—allows them to feel excited, even if they're determined to wallow in discontent. Ma knows how to interact with people. It makes sense they'd want to give her money.

When Dad serves the roasted chicken and risotto, I focus on the tender meat, the rich gravy, and the texture of the delicious food. The whole experience of eating overwhelms me. My mother is telling my siblings how she hired a new writer to help her prepare to meet these big potential donors, but I tune her out as I focus on the herbs and pepper exploding in my mouth. I don't feel concerned about the meeting my mother wants me to attend tomorrow.

I'm no stranger to corporate goals in funding research, and these sorts of meetings are nothing new for me after a decade of high level experiments. I savor the last grain of rice on my fork, closing my eyes to let the flavor linger on my tongue. "Garlic and sage," I mutter, identifying these earthy flavors of home.

When I open my eyes, I see the wrinkled face of Ed Hastings staring at us through my parents' kitchen window. I fly upward out of my seat, startling my sister. Ed snaps a picture with his giant camera as I stomp over toward the door.

"Hunter," my father's voice is stern. "Please don't expose yourself to additional scrutiny." He wipes his mouth with a napkin and cracks open the window. "Ed," he says, his voice calm and stern, as if he's refereeing a fight amongst his children rather than addressing an old busybody he already told to leave. "I'm going to need you to leave my property. I'll see you tomorrow at Tai Chi."

Ed scowls again and snaps another picture through the window as he disappears into the Oak Creek twilight. I can only imagine what nonsense he will print.

6

Abigail

My "interview" with Rose Mitchell is the strangest thing. She hands me a contract to sign and offers me a salary much higher than my father was paying. "Wow," I say, whipping out a pen to sign.

"Abigail!" She scolds and I freeze. "Never accept the first offer without negotiating. Ask me for more money."

I hesitate. I have never met a person like this before. I'm not sure what to do, but I blurt out a number that feels obscene to me. She smiles. "I'll meet you in the middle," she says, writing in the new number and initialling beside it. Once I sign, Rose asks me to help her draw up bullet points and ideas for how to approach her meeting the next day.

I know nothing about drug research or plants or, really, science, but I've certainly helped my father convince large clients to hire his firm. "You want to gain their trust," I tell her, making a list of a few ideas. Despite the whirlwind of upheaval and travel, ideas come to me quickly. I begin to feel like this job was sitting here waiting for me, and I just needed to build up the bravery to come get it.

A few hours later, Rose looks at the clock and says she has to go. "I can fill in the details to flesh out these talking points." She smiles. "Yes, this is going to be fantastic." She starts sliding papers into her bag and looks at me. I'm not really sure what to do. I have nowhere to go… Rose frowns. "Where are you staying, Abigail, dear?"

I shrug, worried for a minute she will drag me home with her. She mutters something about her long-lost son coming home for dinner and says, "Sit tight. I'll send someone to help you." And then she rolls out of the office in a burst of excitement. I stare after her, wondering how I'll ever learn to keep up, but feeling exhilarated at the prospect of trying.

Unsure what to do next, I wander around the office. I've been assigned a cubicle outside Rose's office, with a window behind my seat. It overlooks the lawn, and I'm staring happily out at the golden afternoon light when a sing-song voice echoes through the office. "Yoo hoo!"

Hesitantly, I turn around. "I said 'yoo hoo!'"

The voice belongs to a tiny woman with dark curls and a smile that lights her

16

entire face. "I'm Indigo! Rose said you need me."

I don't even have time to answer before Indigo tells me, in one giant breath, that she runs the Oak Creek Inn, where I'll be staying until I find a more permanent rental. "Come on, Sweetheart," she says, dragging me by the hand. "We'll walk over together and get you situated."

I typically hate pet names. I cringe when men or older women call me Honey or Sugar, but Indigo seems so genuine, like she really believes I have a sweet heart.

Apparently everyone here moves fast, skips over the guarded portion of a relationship and dives right in to sharing their true selves.

I love how Indigo describes the town as we cross under the train tracks to the Main Street that circles the library. "Isn't it just wonderful that the library is the heart of our town?"

I nod, seeing a group of men in sweats doing Tai Chi in the amphitheater next to the library. Indigo tugs me past a tiny market and into a small park flanked by lamp posts that would feel right at home in Narnia.

"And there's the Inn!" She coos. "Isn't that just the perfect spot for an inn? Don't worry." She grabs my arm again. "We have parking out back. You don't have to haul all your bags from the street. I don't tell this to the overnight guests, though. Who needs more than one bag for an overnight?"

The remodeled Victorian house is painted a vibrant indigo and has solar panels clinging to each layer of the slate roof. The charming wrap around porch is lined with white rocking chairs and hanging baskets spilling with bright flowers.

"Indigo," I hesitate, seeing how fancy this place is. "I can't really afford—"

"Nope," Indigo cuts me off. "Rose said your stay should be part of your relocation package to start work at the college. It's covered, girl!"

Relocation package. It sounds too professional for me, like I skipped a few career steps or something.

We walk inside the Inn and Indigo hands me an old brass key. "Room number 8," she tells me. "For luck, although it sounds like you've already got some of that!"

I follow her into the dining room and she slides a plate of muffins toward me, sitting down at the table covered with a crisp linen tablecloth. "So," she says, biting into her muffin and talking with her mouth full. "Tell me everything about you. Rose says you're a writer?"

A writer. As she says it, I allow myself to feel how badly I want it to be true. And maybe it is? If I just signed paperwork for a job with that in the title? I smile, sinking my teeth into the lemon poppyseed muffin. "Well," I say, smoothing my hair so it covers my still-swollen ear. "I'm from Ohio. And I just moved here today." We both laugh at this.

Indigo sits back in her chair and squints at me, sizing me up as if she can see right through me, and maybe she can, because she says, "Tell me about him. We can burn sage later and scrub him right out of your system. You're safe here with me."

I feel the muffin catch in my throat and I reach for the sweet tea Indigo pours as I cough. I've never really had girlfriends before. Growing up, I had my brothers and I'm sort of close with my mother, but she and I sure don't talk about our relationships. There aren't really any women working in Baker and Sons. I'm not used to getting to talk about this kind of stuff. I sigh. "He started out all right," I tell her.

Indigo scoffs at this. "They all do, Sweetheart. They all do." She twirls a wedding ring on her left hand. Seeing me notice it, she smiles and says, "took me awhile to realize I wasn't waiting for Prince Charming so much as *Queen* Charming." Indigo points to a photograph on the wall, where she beams in a white dress in the arms of a woman with short, spiky hair. "My wife, Sara."

They seem so happy in the picture. My eyes well up with tears, thinking that Jack never looked at me that way, especially not toward the end. Especially not that last night. I start to cry and Indigo shifts around the table. "Oh," she says, "It's ok, Abigail. We're going to take good care of you here. You're safe," she asserts again. For a moment, wrapped in her warm hug, I believe it's true.

"I don't even know how things got to be so bad," I tell her, tucking back my hair to show her my ear. I haven't looked at it since I pulled into the parking spot near Rose's office, but it had nearly returned to normal. I was hoping the fear would fade into the background as my body returned to its normal shape, but I still feel myself looking toward each of the doorways, like I'm expecting him to stomp in the room. "The further I drove away from Greenwood, the more I realized how long I've been holding my breath."

Indigo holds my hand and, for an hour, I tell her everything. How I felt like my life was being written by another author, how my family meant well but let their practicality get in the way of listening to my hopes and dreams. I haven't turned my phone on since this morning, but I'm sure I will have missed a dozen calls from my parents, not concerned but calling instead to scold me for not showing up at the office.

When we reach a pause in conversation, Indigo stands and places her hands on her hips. "You know what you need?" I shake my head. "Underpants," she says.

A laugh explodes from my chest, unexpectedly. She's right, of course. I need socks and pants and work shirts. All of it.

"Come on," she says, grabbing her purse and mine. "I'm going to buy you organic drawers from the co-op and then you tell me how much you can spend at the second hand store. We'll get you enough clothes for your first week with Wild Rose."

We walk back through the park and along Main Street. The Tai Chi has given way to marching band practice for the local high school students, whose drums compete with a lone bag piper standing on the hill facing into the sun.

The co-op Indigo mentioned is unlike anything I've seen before. We don't have scarves made from hemp in Greenwood, Ohio, and we don't have multiple types of kale or kombucha, either. I follow Indigo as she sizes me up, shoving a pack of Medium undies my way. "Will they feel…scratchy?" I don't know if I've even touched hemp before.

"Oh! Girl, no. These will feel amazing. You'll probably be ruined for life, even if they look like granny panties." She sees me sniffing the shampoo and grabs a few bottles. She says she needs to restock the inn bathrooms, but I know she's only buying them to be nice. I vow to repay her when I get myself situated.

At the checkout, Indigo introduces me to the cashier. "Mary Pat," she says, "This is ABIGAIL." She emphasizes my name like I'm some sort of celebrity. Apparently, as a newcomer in a small town, I am. "She's going to be working with Rose at the college."

Mary Pat's eyebrows shoot up. "Good luck to you, then," she says as she tucks our purchases into the cloth bags Indigo pulls from her purse. "And did you hear who else will be at the college this fall?"

Indigo leans forward on her elbows. "No!" She gushes. "Tell me everything."

Mary Pat looks around the store, where shoppers are stuffing baskets and cloth bags with vegetables I've never heard of and pies made from foods I never knew could form dessert. She leans in and whispers, "Hunter Crawford. His wife left him while he was in the space station, and I heard he lost his mind and got fired."

"No! Hunter?" Indigo snorts. "His wife was a stick in the mud anyway. He'll get over it." Indigo hands me an avocado "fudge" sample, but doesn't elaborate any more on who this scorned astronaut is.

As we walk back to her place carrying my new undies, I already feel right at home.

"Don't you worry about a thing, Abi-girl," Indigo says, wrinkling her nose at the fake fudge. "We're going to get you sorted out."

7

Hunter

"Not a bad day, brother." Archer crushes a beer can in his hand and tosses it into the recycling bin across the room. His house is tidier than I expected. Growing up, his room was always a cluttered pit. It made me uncomfortable. Now, he has a housekeeper, and I can stand to be in his space without sweating. "You going to drink that?" He gestures toward my untouched IPA.

I sigh and take a sip. I don't drink much, but I guess being back here I break a lot of my own rules. "First the dairy and now the alcohol," I mutter, thinking about how the very first thing I want to do tomorrow is buy workout equipment for my new home.

"You sure you don't want to camp out at your new place?" Archer laughs. He managed to arrange a short sale on a duplex while I helped Ma land funding from the computer engineering company today. Archer prattles on about how skillful he is at negotiating loans and deals, but my thoughts linger on the woman I saw in Ma's office.

There aren't many new people in Oak Creek. Even though I've been gone for years, I still feel quite certain I know almost everyone. This woman, though. I keep circling back to the idea that I must feel intrigued by her because she's new. It's unusual to see someone new, even moreso when I've been living in a tin can in outer space for half a year.

Still. This new woman is objectively, biologically perfect. When Archer snaps his hands in front of my face to ask if I'm listening, I tell him no and go back to cataloguing her features. Wide hips and a round backside...

"Dude, Hunter, you have to either tell me what you're thinking about or else get the fuck out of my house." Archer snatches my beer from me.

"I was thinking about breasts," I tell him, not expecting him to laugh at that. "What?"

"Nothing, dude. I just didn't think you thought about that stuff. I think about breasts all the damn time." Archer scowls. "I'm really sorry about Heather, man."

"Hmph." I snatch the beer back again.

"She...not that I was looking in that way. But Heather had no breasts to speak of."

I tip the beer in his direction. "That's accurate." I take a long sip.

"So you weren't thinking about your wife, then?"

"I was not." Hm. Diana is getting good at making beer. "She wasn't something I thought much about, actually," I admit. I find myself explaining to Archer that Heather made sense. She seemed so tolerant of me in ways I hadn't experienced since moving out from my childhood home. But I have to agree with her assessment that I was a bad spouse. And so was she. If the paperwork from her lawyer means anything, Heather *tolerated* me just long enough to cash in on an investment.

"I don't mind paying her something," I tell him. "Just not *that* much." Heather's alimony request amounts to most of everything I've ever earned, and she even had the gall to ask for a percentage of future patents.

My family recommended a lawyer, Sara Garrett, who helped Indigo with her divorce…and then married her afterward. My expectations aren't high for a small-town lawyer, but Sara seems to be intelligent. "Sara has a plan," I tell Archer. "She also found me a tenant. Said something about serendipitous timing."

I told Sara I'd pay her whatever she wanted to take care of everything for me. Contracts and leases and legal papers. I want someone to manage all these complicated details. I just don't ever have the headspace for that stuff, especially if I'm deep in my research. I should have hired an assistant years ago, rather than marrying Heather. It wasn't fair of me to take advantage of her planning and organizing like that. All I ever want to do is my work.

Thinking of my research reminds me how badly I'm itching to get my lab equipment set up on campus. This, in turn, brings my thoughts back to the new woman in town.

And her biological features. Apparently I still have urges after all. I had briefly felt concerned that my libido had vanished along with Heather.

So this is a positive turn, health wise. Archer and I finish our drinks and I call it an early evening. If I get my act together quickly, I can start my day early tomorrow, set up my stuff in my new house and then spend the afternoon setting up my lab. Soon I'll have everything just how I want it.

Everything except my funding and my career.

8

Abigail

Helping Rose prepare for that meeting was intoxicating. I've never gotten to do anything like that before. She included me in the conversation, too. I had no idea my voice was going to matter. At my dad's company I'm never allowed to do anything different from how it's always been done. File the invoices. Answer the phones. Lots of general office stuff I was happy enough to do, sure. But I just have always wanted to try more, try something different. And, it turns out, Rose asked lots of questions of me about my own college experience to help emphasize the importance of supporting small schools.

I never knew how badly I wanted to get to contribute to something until I got here and started doing it! Rose said the money we landed is called an endowment. I have so much to learn and I feel giddy to get learning it.

I practically skip back to the inn at the end of the day, buzzing with the promise and excitement the future holds for me. I feel called by this place. It's no accident that I stumbled upon this job while I was fleeing a flaming mess back home. I still haven't turned on my phone. I know I need to; my mom must be worried sick to not even hear from me. At least I hope she's more worried than angry.

I stop at the co-op to pick up a snack I can share with Indigo and Sara. I met Indigo's wife at dinner last night. She's as tough as Indigo is warm, but both of them are so kind and welcoming. I feel like I've known them for months, rather than just a day. Has it only been 2 days since I left home?

"Help you find something?" Mary Pat, the cashier I met yesterday, looks up at me from the checkout a few feet away. I've been wandering the aisles daydreaming, running my fingers along the shelves of unfamiliar ingredients.

I chew on my lip and look at her, hopefully. Indigo seemed to trust her the other day, so I blurt out, "I was just looking for something nice to share with Indigo and Sara. I had a good day at work and—"

Mary Pat claps her hands. "Did Rose manage to woo those computer bastards? How many million dollars are they giving her?" She walks out from around the counter and snags a box of gluten-free crackers with flax and sea salt. Stuffing it in my arms, she drags me to the cooler and starts muttering at the cheese selection. "Ah! Here. Come on."

As we walk up to the register, Mary Pat claps another customer on the back. "Matthew!" The tall man with a blond ponytail smiles at Mary Pat as he stuffs packages of jerky in his basket. "This is Abigail! She's new. Working with Rose to woo donations at the college."

I feel like I've been dragged onto an amusement park ride, the way I'm bounced around. Matthew smiles at me, his blue eyes looking friendly as he shakes my hand. "Nice to meet you, Abigail." He leans in and says, "We should talk sometime. I've been trying to get Rose to consider solar panels on some of those south-facing buildings."

Mary Pat clucks her tongue and starts ringing me out. "You get an address yet, honey?"

"Well, I'm still at the Inn."

"Matthew!" She beckons him over. "Let Abigail use your member card. She'll join up when she finds a place to live."

As he hands me the card, he and Mary Pat banter about the changes they'd like to see—solar power at the college *and* more of the buildings around Main Street, different financial donors at the college. Alcohol for sale in town. By the time I leave with cheese and crackers, I've got an invitation to tour Matthew's solar shop and a standing offer to join Mary Pat's book club, which Matthew tells me I can't decline or it'll mean social death for me here in Oak Creek.

He walks with me halfway to the Inn, promising me I can help operate the crane if I come with him to instal solar panels sometime. I marvel again at how quickly this town has enveloped me, like I dropped from the sky to fill a need. But really they're offering me everything I need, too.

Indigo has left a note that she's out running errands, so I stash the snacks in the kitchen and close the door to my room. I can't avoid calling my parents any longer. Sinking into the bed with a glass of water, I turn on my cell phone. Lots of voicemail and text messages. The ones from my father range from "Where on earth are you?" To "what in the hell do you think you're doing?"

My brothers chip in similar sentiments, and my mother leaves long, rambling messages wanting to make sure I've thought things through, brought clean underwear, and considered the consequences of my actions.

I try to erase everything from Jack. There is no concern or regret in his messages. Only rage. He calls me "bitch" and "sneaking liar" in his texts and drunken, slurred voicemail messages. I down the rest of my water and decide to start my calls with my mother.

She picks up immediately. "Abigail! We've been out of our minds with worry."

"Hey, Mom. I'm really sorry I kept my phone off...I..." I drift off.

She picks right up where I stopped, though. "What could you have been thinking? Running off like this without a word? Jack is beside himself."

"He called you?"

"Well of course he called. He came over, actually. Then called the next day when we still hadn't heard a word from you."

"I left Dad a message that I had to get away," I tell her. She spends awhile explaining how much overtime everyone has had to work, picking up my slack around the office. I don't mention that she could have come in to help cover. Mom has been a stay at home spouse since Dad's business got big enough for him to hire outside help. That doesn't excuse me leaving them all short handed, and I apologize for that aspect repeatedly.

"But Mom!" I interrupt her. How do I explain what's been happening with Jack? How he insisted we avoid seeing them and their "charity." He threatened all sorts of things that seemed subtle at the time, but now make my stomach turn. He'd tell me he'd hide my keys if I went to their house, or else slash my shoes with a box cutter. I kept telling myself he was just that embarrassed to be out of work, but I know I should have left long before. I know I'm lucky to get away with just a hurt ear. "Mom, I had to get away from Jack. I just…"

She sighs. "It's not fair to kick a man while he's down, sweetheart."

"This isn't that," I tell her, but she cuts me off again. What must he have told them when he went over there? Whatever it was, he got his chance to make the first impression, and my mother believes I've wronged Jack. Based on what she says, he must have been reflecting his own darkness back to my parents, but placing the blame all on me. If he hadn't been such a monster that night I left, I'd almost feel bad for him.

"When are you coming back? Jack is very anxious for you to come home," she says with a huff. In the background, I hear my father approach, his voice heated as he asks if it's me on the phone.

"That's what I wanted to talk to you about," I say. I curl my hands into fists, balling up the quilt on my bed as I muster the strength to just tell my family what I already know to be true. "I'd like to stay here for awhile. I need a change."

"What?" My father roars into the phone. "Abigail Baker, you get your ass back here right now so we can discuss this face to face. Where did you go? Geneva?"

"I'm in Pennsylvania," I spit out. I'd rather not tell them exactly where I went, I realize, feeling the safety of this small town cocoon around me, like it's Brigadoon or something and I've fallen into a sheltered glen.

"I'm not going to hold your job for you," Dad says. "You've already used up your personal time these past few days and—"

"I got a job here, actually," I interrupt. I hear the sharp intake of breath.

"Doing what exactly?"

"I'm the communications strategist at a small liberal arts college," I tell them, testing out the title Indigo and Sara had suggested for my business cards.

Rose said I shouldn't just call myself a speech writer, since I'd be helping her with much more than speeches. She also said she didn't care what I called myself, as long as I helped her land the big bucks.

"What in the hell does that mean? You have a degree in office management from a branch campus." I know my father doesn't intend to demean my education, but I've had about enough of this conversation. Every day I spend away from Greenwood, I see how much I've let them shelter me, how many of my life decisions were made without my input.

"I actually eked out a minor in professional communication, and today I helped the college president fund an endowment." It feels so empowering to use the phrase Mary Pat slung around the co-op.

24

"Sweetheart, look," my mother chimes in, using her keep-the-peace tone. "Why don't you tell us where you are and we can drive down and pick you up. We can talk this all out on the drive back to Greenwood."

I hear Indigo burst into the Inn downstairs with her now-familiar "Yoo-hoo!" This phone call has reached the limit of what I can handle and I'm eager to tell Indigo about my day, celebrate with cheese and odd crackers. "Mom, Dad, like I said, I'm very sorry to leave you without notice and to head out so abruptly. But I'm going to stick around here and see where this job takes me."

I hear them both inhale to start another tirade, but I decide to cut them off. "I hear someone calling for me, so I have to go. I'll touch base in a few days."

When I make my way into the dining room, Indigo starts telling me all about her errands before she even looks up. "That you, Abigail? Gosh, but I found a steal on these gourds and fall decorations. I know it's still August... We just love fall, Sara and I both. Wanna give me a hand with this garland? I know it's early still and—oh!" She sees my face and drops the bag of decorations, pulling me into a hug. "Come on. Let's go sit and you tell me about it. We need to talk about the place Sara found for you to rent, anyway."

9

Abigail

"I'm just not sure about this," I mutter again as Sara and Indigo toss the last of the housewares in the back of Sara's truck. I can't get past the guilt that I'm taking so much charity from these women, who have already been so kind to me. They barely know me and they're loaning me half the furniture stacked in the basement of the Inn.

Indigo insists it's all been sitting around gathering dust, waiting until she redecorates or has to replace something. "Hush now," she huffs, adding a basket of soy candles and homemade soaps. "Besides, Sara will divorce me if I keep accumulating all these frou-frou smelling things."

Sara nods and ushers me into the cab of the pickup. "She's one hundred per cent correct about that, Abigail. Nobody needs that much jasmine."

Having loaded up my meager and borrowed possessions, we start the short drive around the corner to my new beginning: Sara found a cute little duplex for rent and says the landlord keeps to himself.

I fiddle the shiny set of keys in my lap while we drive, marveling that I've never lived alone before. The truth is I *do* want all those jasmine candles and a dish of pretty soap in the restroom. I want the sage colored hand towels and crisp white linens. I want everything Indigo offered me because I get to arrange it however I want, keep it as clean as I'd like. Or not!

Indigo smiles and hops out of the truck. The duplex is a tidy brick two-story with street parking. Each entry has its own stoop, and I begin to immediately fantasize about putting potted ferns out there. And a welcome mat! I unlock the door and step inside, the smell of fresh paint wafting over me along with the morning sunshine from the front picture window.

"Did you decide which room is the office?" Sara grunts under the weight of the desk she's bringing inside. I get down to business planning out the move. We very quickly bring most of the furniture inside and a few of the clothing bags. I was stunned by how much I could afford from the second-hand store outside town. Indigo knew of a thrift shop where she said all the wealthy college students dump their wardrobes when they graduate and move to more glamorous locales.

As Indigo and Sara heft a mattress upstairs, I walk outside and notice a man peering into Sara's truck. I clear my throat, unsure what to do. Everyone knows each other here, but I don't like the way he's leaning into the truck, running his hands along my borrowed headboard. "Can I help you with anything?" I decide to be friendly in case he's here to lend a hand or something.

I'm not prepared for what happens next. The dark-haired man whips his head up to look at me, brown eyes sharp. "What are you doing with this furniture?" His deep voice is level, measured. He's not angry, I don't think, but he's sure not friendly, either. He looks familiar, but I just can't place him. I've met so many people in the past few days.

"Well..." I don't know how to answer him. His stubbled jaw is set tight and I see him grinding his teeth. Long, lean muscles stand out in his forearms and I watch him grip the wood, lifting it. "I'm moving in," I stammer.

He pulls the headboard up to his face, squints, and says, "Where did you get this?" There's something a bit sad about the way he caresses the wood. He doesn't look up at me as he says, "this is mine."

"Oh." I lean closer to where he's pointing. Someone carved their name into the wood long ago. *Hunter.* Indigo had the headboard in her pile of things she said she'd refinish someday. She talked about etching a stag over the grafiti, neatening up the handwriting. "My friend gave it to me, so I just assumed she—"

"You should never assume." He lifts the headboard fully from the truck and begins to walk toward the house just as Indigo and Sara burst out the front door, laughing.

"Oh! Hunter! Good. You met Abigail." Indigo leans into the cab to snatch the last bag of linens from behind the bench seat. "Glad to see you decided to help with the very last bit of heavy furniture." She swats his arm playfully.

Hunter—I assume that's his name—grunts noncommittally and turns toward the other door of the duplex. Indigo hollers, "Now just a minute, sir. Wrong house!"

"This is a stolen piece of furniture," he says, setting it on the walk. "It's my headboard."

"No, it's Abigail's headboard," Indigo retorts. "Your parents cleaned out that house months ago and I have half the Crawford boys' furniture in my basement. I paid for it fair and square, and I'm giving it to her. Now be a sport and help us carry it inside."

Hunter looks a bit powerless as Indigo pushes him over toward my half of the building and Sara says, "This is the tenant I found for you, dude. Be nice and carry her stuff upstairs for her and maybe she'll water your plants the next time you leave town."

Pausing in the living room, he points his chin toward the coffee table and makes an incredulous noise. "My father made that, too."

Indigo beams. "Well now you can come visit it if you're nice to Abigail. I'll make sure she uses a coaster so she doesn't add any more ring stains to the wood."

He begrudgingly carries the headboard up to my new bedroom and I blush, thinking about sleeping in what was clearly his childhood bed, which he's now seen in a room with my personal belongings scattered around. My landlord, the brooding furniture connoisseur. I get a good peek at the muscular back side of him as he lifts the heavy oak piece into place where Sara has assembled the bed frame. I blush again. I definitely cannot be having these sorts of thoughts about my landlord, especially not in a small town.

The headboard locked securely against the bed frame, Hunter rises, brushes his hands off. He looks at me long and hard, like he's trying to see the cells inside my skin. His expression is utterly unreadable, but he abruptly nods at Sara and Indigo and walks out of the house without a word.

"Don't mind him," Indigo says, pecking me on the cheek. But I didn't mind Hunter. I can't stop thinking about him, actually. Not just that he looked damn good, but he seemed so intense. Like there's so much going on beneath the surface. Indigo backs up to the front door. "We'll get out of your hair and let you get settled in."

I start to protest but Sara claps me on the back. "I don't want to hear another thank you. We are happy to do it."

I twirl a lock of my hair around my finger. I'm still wearing it down even though I think everything looks normal and healthy again. "I just don't know how to repay you," I say, quietly.

Sara pulls Indigo tightly against her side. She gives her wife a squeeze and looks over to me in my own living room of my very own home. "I'll tell you what," she says. "Invite us over for dinner sometime soon and we will call it even."

Tears well in my eyes as they drive off. I'm not accustomed to such genuine warmth and kindness. It'll take me as long to get used to their sunshine as it will to keep up with Rose.

10

Hunter

I can hear Abigail singing in the shower. Abigail Baker.

I looked at the lease Sara emailed me so I could be sure of her name, which is how I also learned that she works at the college. For my mother.

I lie in bed staring at the ceiling, listening to Abigail singing show tunes through the thin walls of the duplex, and take stock of my situation.

My lab, if you can call it that, is up and running. My students start classes today and it's going to take all my energy to be patient with them, constantly reminding myself that they are teenagers eager to learn rather than world calibre scientists with multiple graduate degrees. It all sounds exhausting.

Abigail flubs a high note and I groan, rising from bed to start my day.

I still revel in the readily available fresh fruits and vegetables. After half a year of dehydrated mush, I inhale apples and bell peppers. The crunch and splash of the juice...the pure joy of it overpowers my discomfort at Abigail's off-key singing, which has moved down to her kitchen on the other side of mine.

Eventually I hear her leave her house and, noting the time, I grab my bag and walk to my first lecture of the day. Diana helped me prepare my syllabus and she suggested I start by telling the students about my research in the space station to build rapport. Diana predicted they'd ask me about using the toilet and shaving and sleeping in zero gravity, and I'm stunned to discover that she's right.

It always confuses me to learn that people understand other people, can predict what they will do or say or feel. Other people are such a mystery to me. I am far more comfortable analyzing tissue and vessels. When a student asks the purpose of my research, I light up. This I can do.

"The hope is to develop more effective medications," I explain. "The majority of potential candidates in clinical trials actually fail because the new drugs do not have the intended effect in their body. The more we can study aging tissues, the more accurately we can predict their interaction with chemicals...medications."

The students all seem nervous. *They're worried this class will be very difficult,* I remember Diana had told me. *You intimidate people.* I hold my hands out palms up, a gesture of peace, or so I'm told. "In this class, we will start with cells and once we understand those, we will build up slowly. Maybe we will talk about bones by the end of term." They laugh a bit and I feel relief that I've made a connection.

Maybe this won't be so bad.

My second class goes down in much the same fashion and then, after a few hours in the lab, I walk home eager to work out. We had such limited access to exercise equipment in the space station, and between all the drama with Heather and my job I didn't really get to do much when I got back. A few runs here and there...my body is literally aching to lift weights.

I spent almost all of my personal time in the space station planning out a year's worth of workouts and meals. Digger said it's odd to fantasize about exercise and food while everyone else played cards or read. I realize my meticulous notes about caloric intake versus output are impractical, but I like to aim high.

I made the dining room into my home gym. I don't plan to have guests over to eat and I'm fine eating my meals at the counter or, more likely, sitting at my computer desk, which takes up much of the living room. I tried to explain to my brother that it's my house and I'm going to set it up to meet my needs. Heather always had cushions and decorations all over the place. I never felt comfortable in my house, always worried I'd move something and forget exactly where it was.

I have no desire to use the workout facilities on campus, to wait in line for equipment or overhear undergraduates discussing their conquests while they bulk up their biceps doing preacher curls.

My home gym is my kingdom. I bought everything I need to get a full workout right there. I like to work out without music, to focus on my body and what it's saying to me as I move. I've put in a lot of time studying my biology, figuring out the most appropriate routine for optimum results. I covered the wood floor with thick mats in case I drop a barbell and I hung a pull-up bar on the wall opposite Abigail's half of the house, so it won't make noise. I think I did a pretty good job considering my tenant and her right to peace and quiet.

I arrive home, feeling the warmth of anticipation. Finally—a grueling workout. A chance to burn away everything that happened in Texas, start fresh.

I strip down to my bare feet and mesh shorts so I can concentrate on my form and feel the earth beneath me as I lift the weights. I feel a little warm, so I open the back door to let in the late summer breeze. Soon, I am lost to the beautiful ache of my workout, pushing myself hard.

I am aware that I grunt as I move between exercises, dropping the bar and moving to sets of pull-ups. All my concerns melt away: the worry over my legal situation with Heather. The confusion about what questions my students might ask. Anxiety about how I will find investors to continue my research. All of that is gone—there is only my body and this metal and how fast I can move it.

By the time I'm halfway through a set of pull-ups on the rings, I realize I should have consulted my father about hanging anything from the ceiling. I hear the hardware start to groan as I pull myself up, and then several things happen simultaneously: I curse my failure to plan properly in my excitement, I fall to the ground as the rings give way, and I smack my face on the edge of my weight bench.

11

Abigail

I never had free time in Ohio. If I wasn't at work, I was taking care of Jack or the house...or else hanging out with my mom while she took care of Dad and their house. So when my work day ends here in Oak Creek, I find I've got long chunks of time that are just mine! And I'm still not sure how to fill them.

I decide to do a makeshift spa day at home. I strip down to my undies and a t-shirt to shave my legs, taking my time to hit every crevice and use some of those products Indigo bought me at the co-op. All the different oils in the skin creams feel so nice on my skin.

I move on to a deep conditioning treatment for my hair, leaning over the amazingly deep sink in the vanity in my bathroom. I massage the jojoba oil into my scalp slowly, wondering why I never took time to do this before. I finish the whole thing off with a glorious Turkish cotton towel from Indigo. My god! This towel makes me feel like a princess. Never in my life have I felt anything so luxurious. I make a mental note to buy a set as soon as I can afford it.

I walk to the kitchen looking for a snack, still rocking my turban and hemp undies, and hear something puzzling.

I know the walls are thin. I heard Hunter slamming some cupboards in his kitchen earlier and I flush, remembering my solo concert and realizing he must have heard me belting out the sound track to *Chicago*. But I can't seem to identify the sounds I'm hearing from his side now.

I press my ear to the wall in the kitchen, feeling sheepish, but then I hear a groan followed by a clang. I bite my lip. *Could he be cooking?* Toward the end with Jack, I'd often come home to him slamming the oven, clanging pots around on a wild search for something he never seemed to find. Through the wall, I hear the same sounds of impatience, only with growing desperation.

I start to pace, wondering what to do, if I should call Indigo. *Should I call the police?* I jump when I hear a loud clang, followed by a roar. That just doesn't sound safe.

Then I hear repeated cursing through the walls. "Fuck! Shit. Gaaaaaah!" Convinced Hunter is in danger, I grab the cast iron skillet Indigo gave me and rush out the back door. Hunter's door is open, and my heart races as I step closer. I don't take time to think, just act. I enter his dining room and drop the skillet.

Instead of a dining table and chairs, he's set up weightlifting equipment. Hunter lies on his back, rolling on the ground and clutching his face. I see blood streaming between his fingers, and I run over to him. He looks over at me, eyes wild, and his body stills. I dive into action mode, squatting next to him and trying to nudge his hands away from his face.

"Are you injured?" I peer closer, and see that his nose is bleeding. I jump up and run to his kitchen, in search of towels. Finding nothing, I pull the towel off my head and jog back over to Hunter, who has pulled himself into a sitting position.

I press the towel into his hands and help pinch his nose. "Here, I think you just need to—"

"I know how to stop a nose bleed," he says, curtly.

"Oooh kay then." I rock back on my heels and take stock of the room. There are two holes in the ceiling where it looks like he pulled chunks of the drywall down. There are two ropes coiled on the floor. I can't even think what he was doing when he obviously fell down.

"You're not dressed," he says, not meeting my eyes.

I flush, trying to tug down my t-shirt and cover myself. I look him over and say, "Well...neither are you." He is all lean lines, shining with sweat. His face twists in confusion as he pulls the towel away. The bleeding has stopped, but my towel seems ruined. I wait for him to say something, and when he doesn't, I stand up. My cheeks are steaming hot, and I know I've blushed from my hair down to my toes. Which Hunter is staring at.

"So it looks like you're ok I guess? Do you have any bleach for the towel? I haven't stocked up yet and I'm borrowing it—"

"I will clean the towel and return it to you."

"Thanks." I bite my lip, feeling like this is the strangest first-aid situation I've ever seen, and that's saying something for a girl with 3 brothers and a dad who owns a construction business. To top it all off, I can't stop staring at him. I feel a mix of emotions, ranging from lust to a strong urge to hug this wounded man and make him feel better.

I shrug and bend to pick up the skillet I brought with me. "I'll just let you get back to it I guess." I wish he would say something. He's so intense, the way he trains his gaze on my face without blinking, but doesn't speak. I can feel my heart beat throbbing in my ears under the heat of his gaze. "Bye," I say, backing out into the yard.

As I start to walk home, I catch sight of him bending to pick up the ropes. His muscles strain as he hurls the rope and rings across the room, and I can't help but stare again. He seems carved from stone. My brothers all used to lift weights together. They are all strong as oxen, but thicker. And their muscles are all hidden under a softer layer of cheap beer and Mom's cooking.

Back on my side of the duplex, I decide I have to call Indigo and tell her what happened or else I'll burst with embarrassment.

I try to invite her to go out for a drink, but since she's got a full Inn, she and Sara insist I walk over to their place. "We've got box wine today," I hear Sara yelling.

They both laugh hysterically when I tell them about my foiled attempts at a skillet rescue. At least they don't seem angry about the bloody towel. Indigo pats me on the back and says, "The thing about Hunter is that he takes *everything* seriously. I wouldn't worry about this. He's just...serious is all."

"Who's serious?" A woman shuffles into the dining room, grunting a bit under the weight of a heavy box, which she plunks on the table.

Indigo smiles, obviously happy to see this person. "Your brother, that's who."

The woman snorts. "You're going to have to be more specific."

Sara opens the box and starts pulling out plain brown bottles that I assume are filled with homemade beer. "I don't really think anyone would accuse Archer or Fletcher of being serious," she says. "Abigail here is Hunter's new tenant and she walked in on him with a bloody nose."

"Hmm," the woman sits down and twists off the cap of one of the bottles. "He ok?"

Sara nods and says, to me, "This is Diana Crawford. She makes her own beer and thinks her family doesn't know she grows pot in her office at work."

I reach out for a handshake, and laugh when Diana thrusts a bottle in my hand instead. I use my shirt sleeve to twist off the beer cap, drawing an eye roll from Sara. Diana waits expectantly as I take a sip. The beer is delicious. It's fruity and light, a little hoppy. "Wow," I say. "This is fantastic."

Diana grins. "It's my new IPA recipe," she says, taking a long swig from her bottle. "So tell me how my brother managed to come back from outer space in tact and get a nosebleed in his townhouse."

Indigo pours her beer into a glass and slides coasters toward the rest of us. She fills Diana in on Hunter's "small tantrum" when he saw me taking in the Crawford furniture stash, and I add in that he has no furniture and seems to have pulled down half his ceiling.

"He's probably just angry that his bitchy wife took all their furniture when she left him." Diana shakes her head. "I still don't get why he married her to begin with."

I think about Hunter sitting on the floor, shirtless, muscled, bewildered. I don't like hearing Diana talk about him having a wife. *Huh,* I think. *What's that about?*

"Anyway," she says, "I'll call up Archer to look in on him. Sounds like he needs some Crawford support."

For the rest of the night, we talk about Diana's hops and how Indigo convinced her to get solar panels to power her grow house. "Sar got solar panels at the law office and has an energy surplus," Indigo brags. "Matthew is giddy about it." I settle into my chair, loving the friendly support these women all have for each other, the easy conversation and immediate acceptance they offer me.

Much later than I intended, I wander home and fall into bed, my embarrassment from earlier replaced with deep contentment.

12

Hunter

"Hunter," Archer shouts from outside. "I know you're in there, dude. Come on and let me inside before I scare your neighbor."

I sigh and put down the bag of frozen peas, unlocking the door and returning to my computer desk before my brother makes it inside.

"What the fuck, dude?" He looks around the apartment. I still haven't gotten around to cleaning up the dust and drywall. I've been sucking down ibuprofen and icing my face with frozen vegetables because I don't yet have an ice cube tray.

"I mean…I knew you were living that bachelor life, but this is…what happened to the ceiling?" Archer gestures around the room.

"Gravity," I grunt, plunking the peas back on my nose. "I'm not used to it anymore."

I don't have any other furniture, so Archer sits on my weight bench. He shakes his head. "Do you even have a broom? Of course not. Come on, man. We're going to the co-op. You need to stock up your house."

I sigh and toss down the peas. Archer and I climb into his truck and drive the short distance to the store, with Archer insisting we will need to buy more than two armloads of household stuff. He gives Mary Pat a salute as we walk into the store and grab a cardboard box.

I follow along behind my brother as he tosses things into the box, plucking up a broom from housewares. "Is this made from found materials?"

Mary Pat, hearing me from up front, pipes in, "You're damn right, Hunter! The Acorns have been spending their afternoons making brooms. They go walk the banks of the creek. Real nice craftsmanship, don't you think?"

I grunt in response. The Acorns are a group of Oak Creek senior citizens who never mind their own business.

When Archer seems satisfied, he plunks our purchases on the checkout counter. He grabs the membership application and shoves it my way. "I'm just here temporarily, Archer," I say, frowning.

Mary Pat rolls her eyes and starts laying into me about how the membership discount will pay for itself in just a few weeks of me buying the fancy protein powders she sold me earlier. I can't argue with her math.

I start filling out the form and she leans forward on her elbows. "Ya know," she says, watching as I write in my address. "Technically a duplex is one household. If you catch my meaning."

I pause to ponder what she's just said and I look up at her. "I do not catch your meaning, Mary Pat."

"You really don't know your head from a hole in the ground! I'm saying you pay the membership fee for your household and get a card for your tenant, too. Abigail." She crosses her arms. "It'd be a real nice gesture, is all I'm saying."

Archer laughs. "Yeah, Hunter is the king of nice gestures."

I frown at my brother, but fill out a card for Abigail. Mary Pat is probably just a few years away from her Acorn initiation. I hand her my credit card for all the Castile soap and tea tree bathroom cleaner. I remember the bloody towel and ask, "Do you have something here to remove blood from fabric?"

As we unload our stuff, my brother starts asking me too many questions. He wants to know about my students and my workout. He starts asking about my divorce and, in an attempt to silence him, I blurt, "I saw Abigail without her pants on."

Archer stands up from where he'd been cleaning up plaster dust. "All right. Now we're talking. Spill it."

I explain how I'd failed to test the weight load for the studs where I hung the rings and he throws his water bottle at me. "I don't give a shit about the calculations—though Dad is going to be super disappointed in you. Tell me about your neighbor's panties."

"Well." I'm unsure how to explain what happened. "She heard me fall and I suppose she rushed over to help. She had a towel on her head." I hold up the bloody towel that I'd left on the counter.

"And what did you say? When she rushed in half naked to save you?"

"I observed that she was not dressed."

"Oh my God, Hunter. I cannot with you." He gathers his things and makes his way toward the front door. "Jesus, Hunter. A half naked woman ran into your house. This is such a fucking missed opportunity."

As I sift through the products from the co-op, preparing to soak the blood from Abigail's towel, I think about what Archer said. Missed opportunity. Was he implying I should have...what? How would Archer have gotten Abigail all the way naked? Capitalized on that incident for sex? Could he really be disappointed that I didn't do such a thing? He knows I don't understand women or people at all, really.

I'd like to understand Abigail, though. Every inch of her exposed flesh is burned into my memory. What are the chances she'd ever show it to me again> Leaving the towel soaking in the sink, I head off to bed, wondering how disrespectful it is to dream about my tenant's bare thighs.

I wake up, as usual, to the sound of Abigail singing. I toss her clean towel in the dryer before showering. I estimate that she will head out to work in about 20 minutes, if her routine today is the same as before. Dressing and quickly eating my oatmeal, I grab my bag and the warm towel just as I hear Abigail fussing with her lock next door.

I walk up behind her on her stoop and she startles, yelping as she turns and finds me standing so close to her. "Here," I say, thrusting the bundle toward her. "I cleaned the towel. I've also included a co-op member card for you."

Her jaw drops and I can tell, once again, that I've broken social rules I didn't know about. Studying me, Abigail takes the bundle and quickly unlocks her door. She tosses the towel inside, where it lands on a small table she's set up inside the door. I think about how it would be a nice place to stack mail or set down keys. Abigail seems to be able to plan her house layout for how she lives her life. *Fascinating.*

I realize I'm staring when she coughs and gestures for me to walk on ahead down the porch steps. "So," she says, sipping coffee from her travel mug. It smells strong, and I like the familiar scent. It reminds me of my house growing up, where my parents always seem to be brewing fresh coffee, day or night. "Is your nose ok?"

"What?" I move my hand to my face. "Oh. Yes. It's fine."

I continue walking, and my stride is much longer than hers, so I'm soon well ahead of her on the sidewalk. I hear her yell, "Ok, well I guess I'll see you later?" Her voice goes up at the end, like a question, and I walk into my office wondering how many mistakes Archer would say I made this morning.

13

Abigail

"Abigail!" Rose has taken to bellowing from her office when she has a question. The other women who sit near me all smile. There's a group of staff members who work on the alumni magazine, create all the admissions graphics, and manage the college's website. I love sitting with the creative team, tossing in my ideas when someone wants to talk about the look and feel of a new brochure.

They mostly think Rose is eccentric. I've learned by now to speak my mind with her—she can always tell if I'm holding back. It feels like I've lived here for ages since she's given me so many large projects in just a few weeks. Anna mutters at me to get a move on before Rose really starts yelling, so I grab a notebook and walk down the hall.

"Abigail," Rose says again. She taps a manicured nail against her computer monitor where I see the talking points I sent over for her meeting with a famous author considering a donation. "This is perfection. How much am I paying you?"

"Oh. Thank you. We decided on—"

"Christa!" Rose interrupts with a roar. I hear the office manager approach quickly, heels clacking on the hardwood floor in the hall. "Christa, give Abigail a bonus. She's going to turn this meeting into a funded professorship."

Christa looks back and forth between Rose and me and nods, clacking back down to her office. Rose smiles. "Now," she says, leaning back and pressing her fingertips together. "Tell me how you put together this plan."

"Well, first I read Ms. Bluestein's book and made some notes about her protagonist." I explain how I imagined the author was making meaning of her own experience at Oak Creek College, how it must have been a very formative experience for her. Rose's smile widens as I talk, so I continue. "It really seems like she would want to share that experience with other hopeful writers, and the best way to do that is to make sure they have really good professors."

"We were initially earmarking this donation as scholarship money for summer study."

I nod. "I think we can get that, too, from other sources. But a Bluestein Professorship will touch hundreds of students, offer lasting impact for Oak Creek." I pause. I didn't ask permission to change the gameplan and I worry that people will

37

think I stepped out of my lane. But Rose stands and slaps the desk.

"Come on," she says, slipping off her cardigan. "We're walking into town. This calls for celebratory baked goods."

We step out into the hot afternoon sun and make our way across the bridge over the train tracks that will bring in Ms. Bluestein tomorrow. The rail line parallel to the creek separates the college from the town, and a sweet footbridge connects them. The leaves above the tree-lined walks are starting to yellow. It all feels surreal, magical.

"Where did you grow up, Abigail," Rose asks as we descend the steps onto Main Street.

"Middle of nowhere, Ohio," I say with a smile.

"And you moved here when you saw the job posting?"

I shrug. "It was good timing. I needed a change."

Rose pushes open the door to the Insomnia Bakery and pauses to inhale. Eyes closed, she enjoys the scent of buttery pastry, chocolate delights. A young man with dreads and bags under his brown eyes greets us. "Hey, Rose," he says, slinging a tea towel over one shoulder.

"Abigail, this is Stu. He's got twin sons at home, bless his soul. Is it really insomnia, Stu, if you know it's kids keeping you awake?" She laughs.

Stu shrugs and leans forward. "My wife, Jess, and I sleep in shifts. And work here in the bakery in shifts. And wrangle the boys…you get how it is."

I smile as he pulls up his phone, showing a blurry picture of two little guys running toward the camera, eyes gleaming. "They look like they've got a lot of ideas," I tell him.

"Never fear, Stu," Rose says, tapping her chin. "You'll blink your eyes and they'll be off in outer space or galavanting in France." She gestures at the counter display. "We'll have 2 chocolate croissants, please." Rose grasps my arm, cooing, "There's nothing like a well-made croissant when you're feeling particularly jubilant."

We wave goodbye to Stu and sit at one of the picnic tables in the middle of the town square, eating as the seniors dance their Tai Chi silently. Library patrons weave among them on their way in and out of the building. I've already become accustomed to the way this town just does what it will, follows its heart.

Rose dabs at her lips with a napkin and says, "You're making a difference here, Abigail. I hope you feel appreciated for that." She smiles.

"Oh, I do," I nod, brushing the pastry crumbs from my hand. "I was worried I was overstepping with the Bluestein notes…"

"Nonsense! I told you 1,000 times already. I hired you for your ideas." She stands, tossing the paper from her croissant into one of the nearby public compost bins. "I want you to take the afternoon off. Tomorrow we start preparing for the research symposium and it's going to take all your energy to get the scientists to translate their ideas into something regular people can understand."

She waves, walking back toward campus, and I fight the small moment of panic at the thought of an open afternoon. I remember that Diana said I should drop by the Houseplant Haven any time. I decide to brave a visit, arguing I could buy a houseplant for my new place if Diana doesn't seem like she wants to be social.

A small bell tinkles above the door as I push it open to reveal a store front filled with light and wooden shelves overflowing with all manner of green plants. "I'll be right with you," a voice shouts from the back, so I take a moment to walk around, sniffing the buds and admiring the leaves.

"Abigail! Good to see you." Diana emerges, wiping her hands on an apron and tucking a spade into her pocket. We walk around and she shows me her hops garden, the source of her delicious beer. "Can you keep a secret?" I nod, puzzled, and she says, "I don't show many people my real babies." She beckons for me to follow her into the back of the shop, where an overpowering scent transports me to my brothers' apartment on summer nights.

"Wow," I say, as my eyes adjust to the lights illuminating row upon row of marijuana plants. "What is all this?"

"This is my life's work," she says, explaining that she's in the final stages of securing a license to grow medical marijuana. "I've been working on this strain since graduate school," she says, telling me how she once partnered with neurological researchers in her PhD program.

"Are all the Crawfords biology PhDs?"

She laughs. "No. Just me and Hunter, who does not approve of this work because it's still not legal federally." Diana explains how she meets with hydroponics experts and has a system of koi fish for fertilizer. She shows me some notes about her plants and what they theoretically do differently from other types of marijuana.

I don't understand any of it, but I nod along, easily picking up on her confidence that this is important, to her and the rest of us. I smile, remembering the same passion from Hunter when he speaks up about the biology department at the college. I know he lost his job with the space agency, but he doesn't seem to be wallowing in depression about it. He's moving on, making things happen. Passion seems to run in their family.

Diana asks, "Is it true what Archer says? That Hunter doesn't even have any furniture?"

"Oh." I'm not sure if I should get involved in Hunter's family business, but it doesn't seem too out of bounds to tell Diana that he has a weight room in the dining room and nothing but a computer desk. "And when I saw him, he had had some sort of accident where part of the ceiling fell."

She frowns. "I love him and he's brilliant, but he's totally myopic. Mind if I walk to your place with you so I can check on him?"

"Please do!"

She locks up and we head off down the street. It's nice to walk in step with a Crawford. I giggle, noticing that she doesn't rush on ahead just because her stride is longer.

I enjoy walking with Diana, listening to her talk about her plants, her beer making, her assurances that she's finished with men and all their bullshit. She's so outgoing I start to wonder how she came from the same family as Hunter, who still doesn't smile or talk much.

I follow along as Diana climbs his steps and rings the doorbell. I don't tell Diana that by this time of day, Hunter is usually grunting through an exercise routine. After a few moments of him not answering she leans and peers in his front window. He doesn't have curtains up yet, so we can both see him in the dining room doing squats.

"Oh for Christ's sake." Diana rolls her eyes. "Can you let me in your place so I can go around back and smack him?"

I nod and let her in. She walks through my house muttering about useless men. She bangs out the back door and I see her barge into Hunter's half. I figure they have family things to discuss, so I go upstairs to change into my new post work uniform of leggings and a tank. I'm startled to hear Diana's voice shout up to me.

"Abigail!" I lean out the bedroom window to where she stands in the back yard. Hunter leans against the porch rail, arms crossed over his bare chest. "Wanna come work out with me and my brother?"

I think about how his grunts and clangs have become my sound track while I make dinner, making me feel like I've procured my food from the jungle rather than the Pioneer Woman cookbook.

"Well," I start. "I've never really lifted weights before..." I don't really know if I can be in the same room as him, shirtless, without staring or feeling embarrassed that he saw me in my underwear.

"Come on," Diana shouts. "We'll show you how."

I make my way over there, nervous but not wanting to turn down Diana and risk her thinking I'm rejecting our new friendship. I don't want her to think I'm afraid...of the weights or of Hunter.

Diana grabs a jump rope from a hook and heads out back. She starts jumping rope on the porch and I stand awkwardly in Hunter's dining room, looking around.

He scowls. "You haven't done this before?" I can't get a read on him, but I shake my head. He sighs and hands me a broom.

"Here," he says. "Put this on your shoulders and I'll show you how to squat."

"A broom?"

He nods. "It's best to learn without weight. To make sure you get the motions correct."

I swallow and try to finagle the broom handle so it's resting on my shoulders, but it feels awkward and the wood snags on my tank top.

I feel Hunter's hand on my shoulder, pushing on the broom and trying to bend my body. Every nerve I've got starts to fire, directing wave after wave of sparks through my body. I feel myself break out in goosebumps. I hear him start talking, explaining what to do very calmly.

He's passionate about weight lifting, like he's passionate about everything. His low voice gently talks me through the steps of how to move safely, and I feel mesmerized. He's not a bit impatient, seemingly content to help me get it right. And he keeps his hand pressed against me. I try to focus on his words, but I'm distracted by the heat of his body.

And then, without warning, the weight of his hand on my back takes me back to that night with Jack. I'm transported to the last time a man this close to me, put his hands on my body. My blood runs cold and I spin around.

Too late, I realize I whacked Hunter with the broom stick.

He lets out an "oof" as I drop it. My hands shoot to my face in horror. *Why did my body respond that way?* I look around, seeing Diana's face etched with concern while Hunter mutters and picks up the broom.

"I'm sorry," I say. I walk toward my house. "I can't do this."

"Abigail, wait," Diana says, starting to follow me, but I shake my head.

"I need to go. I'll talk to you later, Diana." I close the back door and turn the lock, sinking to the ground on the other side of the door. I'm so ashamed and embarrassed.

Diana shouts my name a few times, but then she stops and I hear the crack of the jump rope, the clangs and grunts as Hunter continues exercising. I start to cry softly, worried I wrecked my chance at making friends here. I keep making a fool of myself with this family. I spend the night worried my time in Oak Creek so far has been too good to be true, and maybe my landlord will kick me out for hitting him with a broom.

14

Hunter

My colleagues are mostly a group of pompous windbags. None of them have research experience I consider noteworthy. Which I guess is to be expected at a small liberal arts college. The problem is I really need guidance to get started applying for funding. I don't even know which direction to begin—should I be looking to stay at this school and fund research here? Should I be exploring venture capitalists to invest in my research to later sell to industry? I went straight from my PhD program to the space program when they recruited me. Everything I did there was paid for by the agency.

I know that the solution to my problem lies in reaching out to others, but the thought of asking for help just pisses me off. I hate that I have to do this, that all my plans were thwarted. My stomach growls as I leave my second lecture, and I realize I forgot to pack my food today. "Damn," I mutter, changing course and walking to the cafeteria.

I fill my tray with a passable salad and bland chicken. I'm about to carry it all back to my office to eat alone when someone yells, "Oy! Crawford!"

I turn to see Andy Moorley waving at me. I raise my eyebrows, and he shouts, "Come sit, mate. I want to pick your brain." Morley is a transplant from the UK, head of the computer science department. He once had a hot job with a famous tech company, but my mother seemed to indicate he, too, has fallen from grace.

I sit across the table from him and nod. "Moorley."

"The prodigal son returns," he says, talking with his mouth full. I grunt in reply. I regret sitting here. "But really, I wanted to talk to you about a computational biology course this spring."

"That's unexpected." I set down my fork. "Do we do computational biology here?" My masters in that specialty was part of what helped me stand out to the space agency. I suppose it was bound to become more common, but it was cutting edge when I was in my first graduate program.

He shakes his head. "Not yet we don't. But I also know your mum has been bringing in some big name industries lately. With deep pockets." Moorley goes on to tell me about his vision of partnering with big pharma or maybe the military to support his computer science research here and increase funding at the college. I find him to be crass, but I am actually glad I am having this conversation with him.

Until I see Abigail Baker with another man.

They enter the cafeteria together and sit, leaning close together over some documents. I recognize Mark as a high-up employee in the provost office. This meeting is most likely something to do with Abigail's professional work, but I feel my pulse racing and my stomach starts to churn at the sight of them together. *This is a working lunch, that's all,* I tell myself. But I can't look away. She is intently focused on her work, studying the documents and gesturing as she talks.

The longer I stare, the more certain I become that Mark is thinking more about Abigail's biologically perfect features than her words. I grimace as I see him notice her breasts in the conservative blouse she's chosen for work today.

Moorely punches me in the shoulder lightly, and I realize he must have been continuing his conversation about computational biology. "I apologize," I mutter. "Please forgive me."

He turns to look over his shoulder, following my gaze. "Ah," he says. "Mate, do you fancy the bird in the blue blouse?"

"She's my neighbor," I offer, hoping we can return to our discussion. Mark lets his hand linger on Abigail's as they shuffle the documents on their table and I feel an unfamiliar sensation in my chest. What is this feeling? Abigail smiles at Mark, and I decide that she is breathtakingly beautiful, her brown hair the perfect complement to her dark eyes and peach-toned skin. She is also smiling at another man, and I realize the burning sensation in my lungs must be jealousy.

Moorely laughs. "You better make a move with your neighbor soon, then, or someone else is going to."

My eyes snap to Moorely's. "You see it, too? He is attracted to Abigail?"

He laughs at me, causing me to growl in frustration. "Crawford," he says. "Every bloke in this room is attracted to her."

I stand up, abruptly, unsure what to do, but feeling drawn over to Abigail. I walk across the room to where she is sitting and, standing next to their table, I clear my throat.

Mark looks up at me with disdain, but I ignore him. I can see only Abigail, whose face breaks into a smile. She's pleased to see me. The smile reaches her eyes, and I feel warmth spread through me.

"Hunter," she says, still smiling. "I'm glad to see you. I wanted to apologize again about the broom…"

"Oh," I say, shaking my head. "Please don't worry about that." And then I run out of ideas for what to say. It seems like I should not tell her not to get involved with Mark. It seems like a poor idea for me to bring up seeing her in her underwear. Instead I just stand there, studying her face. Trying to learn the lines of her, to see how each facial element shifts with her emotions.

"Maybe we could try again sometime," she says, her voice once again tilting up, questioning.

I start to sweat, and I look over at Moorely, who gives me a thumbs up, staring intently.

"Yes," I say. And then, again, I don't know what to say. So I rap my knuckles on the table.

I note the time and excuse myself, needing to get away and think about what has happened. This is all very uncomfortable and unfamiliar.

I meet with several students panicking about their midterm exam that I haven't even written yet, let alone scheduled, and close my door in relief at the end of the day. I'm off my diet, I've had to interact with new people, I've had confusing feelings about Abigail, and I'm exhausted from all of it.

My office phone rings, and before I finish saying hello, my mother takes off at full clip.

"Hunter, I'm glad I finally got through. Your phone goes right to voicemail. I hope that means you were with students. I'm glad you give your students your full attention, sweetheart."

"Ma," I interject. "Was there something you needed?"

"Yes! Of course!" She sighs. "Your father is grilling tonight. He harvested the whole garden, he told me to say, and everyone is coming to dinner. It's not optional. I'll see you at 6."

Mom hangs up before I can protest. I look up to see it's almost 5. No workout for me today, either, apparently.

I walk directly to my parents' house from work, thinking about my day. Nothing seems to make any sense since I left the space station. I find I crave the routine of each day up there, the predictable schedule and limited social interactions. Here, everything is a challenge. And not the exciting challenge of my research.

I'm deep in thought when I open the back door and am taken aback to see Abigail sitting on a stool at the counter, chatting with my mother.

"Abigail," I say, frowning. "Why are you here?"

She laughs uncomfortably. "I'm having dinner with my boss...why are *you* here?"

My family stares at us in silence. I spit out, "this is my family's house. Didn't you know Rose Mitchell is my mother?"

My parents laugh and apologize for not mapping it all out for Abigail, and my father immediately returns to his explanation of his harvest. "Diana's been helping me with fertilizer," he says, holding up a zucchini the size of my forearm.

I had thought I'd just be among my family, who doesn't ask me to say much and doesn't drain my energy as much as outsiders. With my family, I don't get unexpected reactions to my observations or comments. I certainly don't feel jealousy like I did earlier today when Abigail was merely sitting with a colleague.

My family tells me directly if I've damaged their feelings or said something unkind. Now, with Abigail present, I'll have to think about my words and study everyone's facial expressions to get a read on everyone's mood.

I sigh and step closer to the stool beside her and catch a whiff of her scent. Floating over the basil my father just picked is the very specific essence of Abigail. She smells like the September afternoon. Like fabric softener and the bell peppers she munches.

I decide I don't mind so much if I have to work harder to make conversation with Abigail. I find her...intriguing. This is new.

"Ma kept her name when she married my father," I say. Abigail turns to look at me. "Dad is Daniel Crawford." I point at him and he smiles.

She grins. "This town is so quirky. Now I know to ask who all is related."

Archer and Diana enter through the back door holding a bucket of corn, arguing over something while they sit down to shuck it.

My mother dances across the kitchen to the music on the stereo, and swoops over when she sees them. "Oh good," she shouts. "Everyone is here for the harvest. Diana, did you see the tomato plants? Your father said you helped him keep away all the weevils this year."

Diana waves a beer at me, and I accept it while Archer looks at me suspiciously. I surmise that he's unhappy with me for some reason.

Diana snatches the shucked corn from him and drops it in the giant blue pot beside her. "Arch, did you know Abigail smacked Hunter in the nuts with a broom stick the other day?"

"That is not remotely what happened, Diana." I glare at her, trying to work out whether she's joking. I don't want her to make Abigail feel bad. "The broom bumped my stomach. No harm done."

Diana snorts. "Unlike when you fell and pulled down half the ceiling." She ignores my point and puts a hand over my mouth. "Ma, Dad, did you know your son has no furniture?"

15

Abigail

Dinner with my boss's family is so unlike what I expected. Rose is the exact same person at home—bossy and loud, talkative—but her family is just so vibrant. I'm used to my brothers being so competitive, even unkind to each other. Archer seems to tease Hunter a bit, but I can tell all of them are glad to have him back home and eager to help him figure out how to move on from his past.

The Crawfords all praise their father for his amazing yield. He has utilized almost every inch of their back yard to grow something, and we all dig into the potatoes, tomatoes, corn, and even peaches until I feel like I might burst.

Daniel explains that the olive oil he uses on everything is a special order from the co-op and makes me write it down to ask Mary Pat for some.

"I just want to thank you all for including me at your meal," I tell them. "I love having people to talk to over dinner. I'm not used to living alone." I blush then, and bite my lip.

I don't want to share too much or leave a bad impression. One hand instinctively moves to my ear and, catching myself, I tuck back the loose strands of hair.

Rose waves a hand at Hunter. "You don't live alone," she says. "You live next to Mr. Conversation." Everyone laughs but Hunter, who seems surprised and confused. "I'm sure Abigail can come to you if she needs an ear. Hunter?"

"What?" He looks at his mother, perplexed.

"Well, haven't you and Abigail become friendly, sharing a wall and what-not?"

I think of the half-naked rescue and then about hitting him with the broomstick, and I flush. "Oh, well, I don't want to be a bother," I say.

But then he looks at me, and his eyes bore into mine, and I feel transfixed, frozen by his gaze. I feel warmth creep up my neck. He doesn't blink, but says, "You don't bother me, Abigail."

The room is silent while I let his words sink in. I feel myself melting, hypnotized by those dark eyes.

Diana laughs uncomfortably, but Archer stares at his brother. "Hunter," he says. "Have you asked Abigail about helping Ma secure funding?"

"Oh, I don't think he wants to—" Hunter whips his gaze back toward mine so fast I stop speaking mid-sentence. I watch his face transform into hopeful excitement.

"Of course! You're a writer." He stands. I stare at him, confused. "Abigail, I'd like to discuss my research with you and solicit your advice for my funding proposal."

When I don't say anything, his family looks at me. There is so much nonverbal communication happening, and I just wish someone would explain what's going on. Hunter looks back and forth between his mother and me. "I'd compensate you for your expertise, of course. Is that why you hesitated?"

"I…wasn't expecting you to ask me that," I tell him. "You need help with a grant? I don't know."

"Hunter," his mother pats his arm. "It's late. Abigail needs her rest to work for *me* tomorrow. Why don't you walk her on home? At her pace!"

Before I can process what has happened I find myself bustled out the door with Hunter, my arms laden with leftovers wrapped in beeswax cloth. Daniel shouts after me to wash the cloth by hand in soapy water and reuse it "instead of that awful foil that everyone just throws in the landfill!"

Hunter and I walk in silence, watching as all the shop keepers around the square close up for the evening. Many of them wave and address us by name. Ed Hastings tips his hat at us as he locks the door of the *Oak Creek Gazette* office, a tiny slip of a room between Diana's plant shop and the dry cleaner. I can't help but love the old editor of the local paper, especially after Rose explained that he feels slighted she didn't ask him to help before she offered the job to me.

I watch as Ed studies us walking together, tapping his chin. Hunter greets Ed with a low growl, and Ed turns toward his old car parked nearby.

"So," I say to break the silence as we walk. "Your family is so welcoming. I really appreciate that. It's hard being the new person in town."

Hunter doesn't respond for awhile, but finally says, "I'm not good at interpersonal interaction."

"Oh. Well…"

"People think I'm angry. I rarely am. I just don't understand what other people are thinking."

"Oh. Ok, well…"

We stop at an intersection and he looks both ways, which I find endearing because there's not a soul or a vehicle in sight. He continues, saying, "I'd appreciate it if you could tell me what you are thinking when we are with one another. Please don't assume I know."

I nod. "Ok. I was thinking that you seemed excited when Archer asked about my work."

"Yes," he says, his voice taking an animated turn. "Very much so. I need—would you mind coming in so I can show you something on my computer?"

"That's fine," I say, setting my leftovers on my stoop before following him in his front door. I notice that he doesn't look behind him to make sure I've come with him. He's already seated at his computer, pulling up files.

"These are my research notes," he says. "They only make sense to me, and I don't know how to do proposal writing. I'm told it's a different skill? My work is about my data…I need someone to help me *sell* my ideas. To a buyer," he adds, which makes me smile. "I can't tell if you are smiling because you are happy about this idea or if you are mocking me."

I look around for somewhere to sit, but finding no other furniture I just lean back against the bare wall. "I was smiling because I can tell this is important to you, and I find it refreshing that you are so blunt about what you need help with, even though you are, like, a brilliant astronaut. And also, that you think I can help, because I'm just some girl from Greenwood, Ohio."

"I don't think your geographic origins affect your communication skills," Hunter says.

"Well, my father would tend to disagree." The last time I'd spoken to my parents, after they finished pleading with me to come to my senses, my dad began to holler that the fancy college people don't give a shit about the words anyone from Greenwood has to say or write.

I wish so badly I had the strength to defend myself to him, to use my words with my parents and help them see why I had to leave. Maybe I'll never get strong enough to say those things. But maybe I can become another kind of strong—strong enough to fight off any man who lays his hands on me in anger.

I look around Hunter's weight room and think about him working out every day over here. I pull myself back to standing and put my hands on my hips. "I want to learn more about your project. We can work out a barter."

Hunter scans his downstairs, barren save for the free weights and his computer gear. "Barter for what?"

"I'd love it if you teach me how to get strong."

16

Hunter

Abigail is supposed to come over after work to start our barter. I promised to teach her some basic weightlifting techniques and she's going to help me sort out some funding applications. She did mention that it's up to me to make the contacts and set up meetings, which gives me pause. My brother Archer says I need to find a hustler if I want to branch out on my own.

Abigail thinks I can land research funding to stay at Oak Creek College, and maybe even stop teaching. Just work there as a researcher professor.

I'm very eager to begin our trade. I'm not sure whether we should work out first or get started talking about my project. I feel a buzzing energy at the thought of moving forward with my work, an equally present fear that I won't be able to communicate my needs clearly enough to interest an investor.

I see Abigail approach the back door and open it as she raises a hand to knock. I have to remind myself to focus on her eyes and not to stare at her luscious body. I can't help but notice the rounded curves made visible by her tight workout gear. It occurs to me that she will get sweaty, and I hadn't realized the thought of a sweaty woman would be so alluring. *Focus on her eyes,* I remind myself before my thoughts get away from me.

"Hey," Abigail says, smiling. "I brought a chair." I brave a quick look down to see she's holding a camping chair. It looks new, and I feel a wash of guilt that I hadn't thought to go buy a chair, since I knew I'd be having guests.

"I'll reimburse you for the cost," I say, but she laughs.

"Your mom gave me a bonus. Besides," she plunks the chair over by my desk. "Now I have somewhere to sit for the Autumn Apple fireworks." Abigail places a water bottle on the counter and asks if we can start with our workout. "I think it will help me focus on all your big science lingo if we exercise first."

With a nod, I reach for the broom stick. "It's important to learn how to safely move through the exercises before you add weight," I tell her.

"And safely hit you in the guts with the stick?" Her eyes twinkle a bit when she asks this, so I feel certain she is making a joke about our last encounter. I just nod.

I show her how to thread the dowel across her shoulders and grip the handle. "Now," I say, "the most important thing is to arch your back as you bend your knees." I see her watching me intently as I demonstrate the motions. I like having her eyes on me like this and I realize I'm feeling comfortable around her. That in itself is unusual. "You look like you'd like to ask a question," I say, putting down the broom.

"How come you are always barefoot when you're working out?"

"Oh." We both look down at my feet. I wiggle my toes. "It helps me balance and make sure I'm distributing my weight evenly when I move."

Abigail nods and stoops, beginning to untie her shoes. My breath catches as I see the line of her cleavage at the neck of her tank top. Her breasts are magnificent. She tosses her shoes to the side and extends a hand for the broom. Our fingers brush together as she takes it from me, and I feel as though she's rubbed a raw nerve. The contact pulses through my body, catching me totally off guard.

Prior to this, I had only read about such things. I never experienced a physical yearning like this. *How remarkable,* I think, wanting to touch her again to see if the zap returns.

I stand back as Abigail adjusts the broom stick across her shoulders and arches her back. "Like this?" She asks. I nod, watching. It feels strange to be invited to observe her so closely, and I have to remind myself I'm supposed to watch her form, to keep her safe so she doesn't strain or injure a muscle when she adds weight. As Abigail bends her knees, I see her spine curve and I extend my hand to make a correction.

"Abigail," I clear my throat. "Would it be all right if I put my hand on your back so you can feel how to move?"

"Oh." She swallows. "Yes. Thank you for asking first." I stretch open my fingers and place my palm on her back. I can feel the heat radiating through her shirt, and am relieved, thrilled by the tingle that climbs up my arm upon contact. Her body molds to my touch as she bends, her form perfect.

"That's excellent," I whisper. I hadn't intended to whisper, but I find that I cannot concentrate when I am touching Abigail's body. "Do you feel the difference?"

She seems breathless and nods, continuing to move through the exercise until I withdraw my hand. Abigail swallows. I can feel my heart pounding as if I had been working out, and I tell myself it's because I'm working so hard on my social interactions. It's always an exertion for me to be near people, especially new people. "Do you think I can add weights?" She looks at me hopefully. "I want to get strong as quickly as I can."

"The only bar I have weighs 45 pounds. We could try that and see if it's too much." I help Abigail position the bar across her shoulders, feeling small zaps and jolts as my knuckles graze against her skin around the tank top. Evidence suggests I am physically attracted to Abigail, and I'm not sure what to do about that.

"Ok," I say. "I'm going to put my hand on your back at first while you've got the weight on."

"Got it." Abigail bends her knees slowly until her thighs are parallel with the ground and she grunts a bit as she starts to rise back to standing. She laughs. "Oh man," she says, leaning into my palm a bit. I feel her ribs expanding and contracting as she breathes. "Now I see why you make so much noise when you do this."

I smile, even though she hasn't said something amusing. I feel a deep yearning to touch her more, but also to watch her move, to see her delight in achieving something difficult.

I coach Abigail through a few more sets of squats and then show her a basic deadlift. She has a harder time with the proper form for a deadlift, even after watching me and feeling my hand on her back. "Could you take a picture of me so I can see what you're talking about?" Her question makes me feel foolish. If we were in a gym, we'd have mirrors to use as a tool so she could see her form.

"That's a good idea," I tell her, reaching for my phone on the counter. I set up the camera and tell her to try again, snapping a few shots as she moves. "Hey," I say as she executes a perfect lift. "You did it! Here, look." She puts the bar down and we lean over my screen. "See how your back looks different on this last one?" Abigail nods, smiling.

She fans herself and looks away from the photos. I'm relieved when she asks if we can call it a day. Somewhere along the way, I developed a raging erection from watching her move.

17

Abigail

I limp over to the bag chair and collapse into it. I shouldn't be this tired after just a few exercises with light weight, but my body is screaming at me. I lean my head back against the wall, breathing heavy, but then I feel Hunter staring at me again and open my eyes. "What?"

"You didn't stretch," he says. "Your body will build up lactic acid and you'll be sore if you don't stretch."

"Won't I be sore anyway?"

He ponders this a minute before replying. "Yes. That's likely if you have no experience lifting weights. I must recommend that you stretch, though."

"Hunter, I'm not going to move from this chair for a bit. If you want to stretch, suit yourself." As he bends and twists his body, I enjoy the view. He doesn't have a spare ounce of flab. I think about my own soft stomach, the way my thighs slide together while I walk. Maybe lifting weights will change all of that. I think about Hunter touching my back, how my skin seemed to ripple beneath his fingers.

It's just been awhile since I've been with a man, I convince myself.

I don't want to get involved in a relationship, especially not with my landlord. My boss's son. That's not why I came here. *Better change the subject,* I think.

"Tell me about your project," I say, turning to look out the window as Hunter bends to touch his toes.

He grabs a glass of brown liquid and sits next to me at his computer desk. "I took human tissue samples with me to the space station," he says, pulling up some images on his computer. "I am doing my best to explain this in lay terms. I practiced last night." He looks at me as if he's frightened I might run away.

"I promise I'll interrupt you if I don't understand," I say and he nods.

"My research was funded jointly by the institutes for health and the advancement of science. I was using my computational background to study and understand how gravity, or the lack of it, affects the tissue. The goal is to see what that means for disease and human health."

"Wow. It's so amazing to me that you're my landlord and you've just, like, been to outer space."

He blinks and scowls. "Should you be taking notes?"

"I'm good. Tell me more." Hunter shows me how his tissue samples changed quickly in space and how he believes this is a model for how disease might slowly affect people's tissues on earth. I have to interrupt him a few times when he starts explaining how vessels in bones behave differently from those in organs. "It sounds like your research requires you to be away from gravity," I say, hopeful that I'm understanding him. "Can that be done without being in space?"

Hunter frowns. He's quiet for a long time, and I'm worried he's angry that I don't understand what he's talking about, but then he says, "that's the crux of it, Abigail. We weren't finished studying the samples yet, and they canceled the program."

"So what are you trying to do? Build another space station and try again on your own?"

He frowns. "I just need someone to fund a mission back to the existing space station," he says.

I pull out my phone and tap into the web browser. "So…you need 58 million dollars?"

"Approximately."

I sigh. "Do you have anything to drink? I feel like I need one of Diana's beers."

Indigo calls a while later, when I've limped home and collapsed on the couch. "Ungh," I groan by way of greeting. "I think my legs are on fire."

"What on earth have you been up to over there?"

I tell her how I decided to start lifting weights and she cuts me off. "Get your ass over here. This sounds like an in-person kind of story."

It takes much longer than it should to hobble slowly to the Inn, where Sara and Indigo are helping an elderly couple out to their car. "You all simply *must* come back this spring for the May Day festival," Indigo coos, tossing a suitcase into the back seat. "I'll save room number 6 just for you." The woman pats Indigo's hand while her husband fires up the engine of their ancient Cadillac. Sara drapes an arm loosely over her wife's shoulders as I make my way toward them.

"Eesh," Sara says, frowning. "What the hell happened to you?"

"Exercise," I moan, hobbling up their porch steps. We walk back to the living room, and Sara pulls out a tennis ball.

"Here," she says. "Lie down with this under your back and wriggle around. It'll help, I promise."

Indigo runs off for a tray of snacks as I roll around on their carpet.

"I brought cucumber water for us," Indigo says, scooting up closer to her wife on the couch. I force my aching body to get up and into a chair opposite them and chug the water.

"I should have listened to Hunter and stretched," I moan.

"Wait," Sara stops mid-sip of her chilled cucumber water. "You were lifting weights with *Hunter?* Like, socially?"

Indigo passes me another mason jar of water when she sees I've finished mine. "Abigail here was about to spill her guts," she says, pulling up a basket of popcorn. "I always like snacks for a good story. Now. How did you wind up lifting weights with Hunter Crawford?"

Sara rolls her eyes, but helps herself to a handful of the popcorn. I tell them about dinner and our barter. Then I bite my lip and reveal, "and he lifts weights with no shirt on."

"Ooh, this is juicy," Indigo says. "So you're working out to shape up for a good shag?"

I explain that I can't explain why I want to learn to work out. Sara interjects, "Well a half naked man will help. If you're into that."

I throw a piece of popcorn at her, but admit that shirtless, intense Hunter is definitely a perk. "He's like an iceberg," I tell them. "I think there's a lot of interesting stuff going on beneath the surface." By the time they each tell me what they know about him—not much, considering they've known him for years—I'm too sore to walk home and they put me up in one of the guest rooms for the night.

I walk into work the next day feeling lighter and stronger. I dive into writing remarks for Rose to host a fancy pants investor looking to help the undergrads form their own startup companies. Oak Creek College is a short train ride away from New York City and Philadelphia, and our students are filled with all sorts of interesting ideas for tech companies and smarter mass transit.

They've got ideas for apps and robots and all sorts of things.

I text Hunter to tell him about this one visiting investor, Asa Wexler. He seems like the kind of guy Hunter should meet, and he's coming to town later this semester to meet with Rose about funding some chemistry initiatives. *Come check out this guy's investment portfolio when you get a chance.*

I feel pretty proud that I retained everything Hunter told me about his work and located an investor prospect from this list. Asa's interested in pharmaceutical research. Based on what Hunter has said, I have a feeling this will be a good connection for him.

I'm jolted out of my thoughts when I hear a chorus of laughter erupt from Christa's cubicle. All the women from my floor are gathered around her computer howling, dabbing at their eyes. I must have been deeply engrossed in my work to miss what got them to this state. "What on earth is going on over there?"

Christa beckons me over. "Ignore the illustrations," she says, pointing at an article on her monitor. "Or don't. Your mileage may vary."

I squint and lean in to see they're all cackling about an article proclaiming there's a new technique for going down on a woman.

"Guaranteed to deliver orgasm in under three minutes." I feel a flush begin in my chest and spread upward to the tips of my ears. As Christa and Anne gush about how their boyfriends do just fine without this new technique, I can't help but remember how reluctant Jack was to try anything adventurous.

I'd had other partners before him, but in the years between high school and Jack, nobody was doing anything mind blowing. With a sigh, I read along about this so-called Kivin method until I hear a voice over my shoulder.

"Biological approach to stimulation of the vulva. Fascinating."

18

Hunter

My arrival seems to have startled Abigail. I make note that I should announce my arrival before approaching behind her. The women seemed very engrossed in the article on the screen, and upon reading, I can understand why.

When Abigail turns to face me abruptly, I explain, "There's long been discussion of the male climax as a biological response to stimulation, while the human female climax is thought to be equal parts physical and psychological. This article suggests a method of a biological female orgasm. Purely a result of proper stimulation technique. Fascinating."

"Is this guy for real?" Abigail's co-worker addresses her question toward the group at large. I frown, realizing I must have committed a social mistake, verbalizing my thoughts on the article.

Abigail stands and introduces me, saying, "This is Dr. Crawford from the biology department. He takes a professional interest in how tissues react to stimuli."

I feel an odd sense of warmth and delight at hearing Abigail summarize my thoughts in a way that seems pleasing to the other women. They smile genuinely and return to their work areas. I follow Abigail to her desk, where she pulls out a folder about the investor she mentioned. "I wanted you to check out his other investment interests," she says. "He's coming to campus anyway, so we may as well try to set up a meeting for you."

"This does seem promising," I tell her, noting the list of start-up companies he's nurtured, then sold to larger corporations for a hefty profit. Asa Wexler must be a billionaire. "He invested in the new Lyme vaccine," I say, impressed.

Abigail smiles up at me, and again I feel the warm sensation of pleasure course through my body. She seems about to say something when I hear my mother shout for Abigail to come to her office. "We can talk about it after work," Abigail says, rising and smoothing the sides of her skirt.

I watch her walk down the hall, noting the beautiful shape of her backside, and remembering how her bare legs looked in my house. I have to remind myself that I'm just having a natural, evolutionary response to her. Pair this with a discussion of orgasm, and it makes sense that I have another throbbing erection.

All afternoon, I try to focus on my lecture and my students, but I am distracted alternately by memories of the magazine article and of Abigail, translating my thoughts into phrases other people enjoyed. *Does she understand me?* She seems to.

Nothing seems to shake me from my distraction, not even poring over my microscope or diving into my statistical software. I go home early to get a good workout in before helping Abigail work slowly through her repetitions.

Her deadlift and squat technique has improved dramatically, and she has been able to add more weight to the bar than I would have thought.

Her skin shines with sweat as she finishes a set of ten lifts and then she walks over to add more weight. Watching to see that she attaches it safely to the bar, I see that her nipples have hardened visibly. *That's a normal side effect of exertion,* I think, coughing and adjusting my shorts. *This doesn't mean my tenant is aroused.*

"How long until my muscles are as defined as yours?" Abigail pokes at her legs. I know from the few times I've placed my hands on her body to correct her form that Abigail is primarily a soft person. Warm and smooth, her body often quivers beneath my touch, as if I could drown inside her curves.

"I have slow twitch muscle fibers, with a great deal of adenosine triphosphate production," I tell her, unable to look away from her nipples.

"Adenosine? Can you dumb it down for me a little?"

"I estimate that your body is composed of fast twitch muscle fibers," I tell her. "I think you have the ability to get very strong and produce a great deal of force, but might not be predisposed to long duration endurance activities."

"Hm." Abigail frowns and pauses in preparing her exercise. She's quiet as she carries out her repetitions, which is uncommon for her.

"Did my assessment upset you? I frequently upset people inadvertently. I assure you, I placed no value judgement on either muscle type…"

She offers a slight smile, her face unreadable to me unless I study. Are her pupils contracting? Is her breath increasing? The pulse points in her throat? I can never answer anyone quickly, because it takes me a good deal of time to study their biological markers and calculate which emotion they are likely experiencing.

"I see that you are flustered," Abigail says. She shakes her head. "You didn't upset me talking about my body." She grins. "I know I'm a thick gal."

Grunting, Abigail lifts the bar and then pulls it up to chest height. She lowers the weights to the ground and says, "No. I was feeling a little homesick I think. My brothers all lift weights together. Not that they ever invited me…"

"Diana didn't allow us to exclude her from our activities," I observe. We both share a small laugh about that, and she finishes her workout. Abigail leaves her camping chair in my apartment, so it's all set up for her to sink into it when we're done. She continues to refuse to stretch after our workout. "I don't understand why you would choose not to take care of your muscles properly after exercise," I scold, handing her a glass of chocolate milk.

We've developed a routine where I talk about my work and she types notes into my computer, emailing them to herself to make sense of when she has time to ponder them. I hate having someone else touch my computer and it's frustrating to have these limitations. My patience for teaching her to exercise seems endless, but I do not approve of her process at all for putting this proposal together.

As Abigail struggles to type her password into the dual-authentication system I set up for her cloud storage, I can't take it anymore. I snap, "We cannot continue in this manner, Abigail. When will you get your own computer?"

Even I can read her frustration as she looks over at me. "I had a laptop and my asshole ex boyfriend broke it. I'll get a new one when I can afford it, Hunter." Her tone is harsh, but I'm distracted by her use of the word broke. Not disabled or erased or corrupted.

"Define broken," I say, crossing my arms and leaning back in my office chair.

"He smashed it…like bent it backwards the wrong way…" her voice is soft. This man sounds decidedly unpleasant and I don't like that Abigail was romantically involved with someone who would do such a thing.

I think of my conversations with Moorely. We often brainstorm as he tinkers with various hardware he has rescued. His students are always coming to office hours with odd bits and pieces of computers and they cobble together machinery capable of fantastic computational speeds. "Do you still have this laptop?"

Abigail invites me to follow her into her side of the duplex while she fetches the broken computer. As per usual, I forget social conventions and follow her upstairs as she retreats to her bedroom closet. She starts as she realizes I'm still behind her when she stoops to pull a box from the closet. She places a palm to her chest. "Hunter, you move so quietly. I didn't know you'd followed me."

"Bedrooms are a private space." I recite some of the social rules my father used to tell me I needed to memorize whether or not I understood their purpose. "I apologize for violating a custom."

"Next time I'll make sure I clarify. Hey, do you want to visit your old headboard?" Abigail's laugh seems to be the nervous type of laugh. I glance over to her bed, which she's decorated with blue checked sheets and a white puffy duvet. The dark wood stands out in contrast to the walls she's painted a soft blue. This seems like a pleasant space to sleep and wake up each morning.

Then I look into her arms, where she's holding a cracked laptop case. "May I ask what inspired you to keep this if you were certain it was irreparably damaged? From Indigo's description, you brought little else with you from Ohio."

Abigail bites her lip and tucks a lock of hair behind her ear. The gesture is alluring to me. I like standing close enough to watch her chest rise and fall with her breath. "I don't want to lose my novel," she says. She sinks onto her bed, sitting at the edge with the broken laptop in her hands. She tells me how she began working on a creative writing early in her college career and had a working draft of a novel nearly complete when her ex-lover destroyed her computer during an argument.

Even though I haven't been invited to sit, I do, holding out my hands for her to pass over the laptop. Upon brief inspection in the fading light, it would appear the portion of the laptop containing the hard drive is in tact. "Abigail," I meet her gaze. "I might be able to extract the information from his hard drive."

Her eyes well up with tears. I develop a stress response and wonder what I said to make her cry. I run through a checklist. I was kind. I hadn't commented upon her appearance…*what are all the reasons women cry?*

"Oh, Hunter! I can't believe you would do something so kind for me." A single tear rolls down her cheek, captivating me. When I look closer, I see that Abigail's pupils have dilated. She has leaned closer to my body.

"It stands to reason that your novel was of high quality," I tell her. "My mother describes your writing as excellent and I have seen evidence that you have strong communication skills." My words seem to reassure her and she lowers her head, flushing.

"Thank you," she whispers. Her scent fills the room. I can smell the fresh, soapy, rosemary essence of her permeating the sheets. It's an intoxicating aroma, even with the edge of sweat from her workout. I acknowledge that I am very aroused by Abigail. This is all very new. I hadn't been thinking about women...had only focused on my failings as a scientist since returning from space.

It has been many years since I entered a relationship with a new person and Heather took the initiative when we began dating. Abigail and I have become friendly, exchanging jokes and talking comfortably in my house most days. It is not out of the question that she might share an attraction to me. I run through the biological signals someone might use to make their attraction evident. Flushed skin, rapid breathing, dilated pupils. Abigail leans closer to me and I nod, swallowing. *Yes.* I decide. *She would like me to kiss her.*

Shifting my weight to my right hand, I lean closer to her and raise my left, bringing it to her cheek. I want to repeat her gesture of tucking her loose hair back and out of the way, and I'd like to stroke her cheek. She breathes through her nose, meeting my gaze as the pads of my fingers make contact with the sensitive skin near her ear. In slow motion, gently, I begin to tuck her stray lock behind her ear, but Abigail stiffens and pulls back.

19

Abigail

Damn my traitorous body! Damn Jack to hell for making me scared, question my instincts. Just as Hunter leaned in for a kiss, I froze and recoiled from his gentle touch.

He leaps from the bed, snapping to attention. "I apologize, Abigail. I misinterpreted your biophysical signals."

Hunter turns abruptly to leave and rushes down the stairs.

"Hunter! Wait, please let me explain!"

He pauses midway down the stairs, but doesn't turn to face me. I cling to the bannister above him. "You didn't misinterpret. I wanted you to kiss me. I just don't know if I can."

He slowly turns to face me, frowning. "I don't understand."

"I just…I might be broken."

He shakes his head, but ascends the stairs to stand closer to me. "I don't believe you could be broken, Abigail. You seem very functional to me."

I exhale slowly, my cheeks puffing out as the breath leaves me. "Will you have dinner with me? Let me tell you what happened before I came to Oak Creek."

"I'm following a careful diet regimen."

"So you don't want to keep talking to me?"

He shakes his head and runs his hands through his hair. "That's not what I mean. No. I mean yes—I want to talk to you."

After some nudging, Hunter explains that he's worried his pre-planned food will spoil if he doesn't eat it today. He brings his food over to my house, and sits while I make my own fresh dinner.

I can't help but smile at how fastidiously he pays attention to what he eats. He's so careful about everything. It must have taken a lot of courage for him to lean in for a kiss. I feel terrible that he must have been running calculations, trying to decide whether I'd welcome his touch, only to have me jerk back as he delivered a gentle caress that should have warmed me to my bones.

We sit in companionable silence, eating, until he says, "Judging by the trauma to your computer and the haste with which you departed Ohio, I have deduced that this Jack person harmed you physically." When he looks at me, his dark eyes have a hard edge. I've never seen him look like this. "If this is accurate, it will take some time for me to manage my anger."

I nod. I summarize my relationship with Jack, how his layoff was a catalyst for his descent into anger and deeper depression. "Not like you, Hunter. I admire how you don't let anything get in the way of you pursuing your passion."

When I talk about the night I left, I see Hunter swallow and grit his teeth. "Abigail," he says, his voice rasping. "I both want to hug you and harm Jack. May I hug you?"

"Oh, Hunter. Yes, please." I lower my hand into his on the table, squeezing. He catches me off guard when he stands and tugs me gently to my feet, enveloping me in his long, muscular arms. He pulls me close against his body until I can feel him inhale and exhale, feel the gentle throb of his heart. He hugs me without ulterior motive. Just wraps his arms around me and rests his chin on my head. His large hands splay wide across my back and press me against his body.

It's been a long time since I've been held. This is an extended embrace, a spoken desire to comfort me, from a man who doesn't speak much about his emotions. I start to cry, and let myself weep out all my frustrations while Hunter just holds me and breathes with me. I cry for all the time I've missed with my family and cry from the ache of them not coming to my aide. "I feel so many conflicting emotions," I murmur against Hunter's t-shirt.

"I often feel emotions are conflicting," he says, which makes me laugh.

I pull back and start cleaning up the supper dishes, startled to see Hunter helping me. Growing up, my brothers always left the table straight away to help my father with some household chore or another. Cleaning out the gutters. Mowing the grass. Tinkering with the boiler in the winter. Dishes and kitchen work were the realm of my mother and me, and so it went when I lived with Jack. I never felt resentful of it. After all, I had no desire to mend the alternator on the lawn mower.

There is something so heartfelt about Hunter loading my dishwasher, just automatically helping me tidy my kitchen. I feel a rush of desire overtake my body so rapidly I have to grip the counter to catch my breath. "I wish my parents had noticed I was floundering," I tell him, trying to take my mind off the way it felt when he held me. I can't stop the flood of thoughts I'm having now, staring at how his mesh shorts drape from his ass.

He seems to consider my words and tells me, "My parents notice everything. Regardless, they did nothing to prevent me from marrying a person who would try to take my intellectual property." He pours the powdered soap into the tray in the dishwasher and presses start. "My father says that children need to be allowed to make mistakes and learn from the consequences of their actions."

This makes me sigh. "I still get the sense your parents took all your wants and needs into consideration when guiding you through your life choices."

"That's an accurate assessment," he says. He looks up at the clock above the sink and coughs. "I need to be going now. I believe it's customary for me to ask if there's anything additional I can do for you."

Kiss me, I think. *Press me up against the fridge and kiss me until my lips are swollen.* But I don't say that. I just shake my head and thank him for being a good listener. He grabs the shattered laptop and walks out the back door, reminding me to lock behind him and ensure the security system is activated. When I climb in bed later, I dream of Hunter Crawford's arms around me, strong and silent.

20

Hunter

"Moorely, I have a favor to ask of you."

"Whatcha got, Crawford?" He sits back in his office chair, arms crossed, eyebrow raised. I deposit the remains of Abigail's laptop on his desk with little fanfare. He squints and picks up the pieces. "What the hell happened here?"

"Are you able to extract the files from the hard drive? I would be grateful." I wait while he examines the pieces for a few moments. He sits up and raps his fingers on his desk, gazing at me with an unreadable expression.

"This is no problem," he says and I relax a bit. Abigail will be extremely happy if I can give her back access to her novel. Making her happy feels like an enticing objective.

"Well, thank you."I start to walk out of his office, assuming he will contact me once he has achieved his goal.

"Well, now, hang on a minute, mate. It'll cost you."

"I thought you just said it would be no problem?"

"That doesn't mean I'm going to do it for nothing! I need you to come with me to play cards this Friday."

I spin around in the doorway to study his face and determine whether he's joking. I see no signs of a smile, no indications around his eyes that he might be teasing. "You play cards?"

"Crawford," he sighs. "I play cards about as well as you tell jokes."

"Surely you are able to just assess the numerical probability of each outcome and bet accordingly?"

He shakes his head. "I don't know. I'm just not good at it. I'll trade you this hard drive excavation for a night of poker and booze."

"Is the alcohol mandatory? I'm balancing my caloric intake now that I've re-established a routine here—"

"Jesus, man. You don't have to take a drink." He sends me a calendar invite to his card game and tells me to bring my brothers if they're in town. As we walk to lunch he elaborates, explaining that he's lost quite a bit at this particular card game over the past few months. When I look at the invite, I note that the list includes a group of retired academics and local business owners.

"Moorely," I begin. "Have you been playing cards with the Acorns?"

A flush creeps up his pale cheeks and he hangs his head. "Crawford, mate, I don't know what the hell happened."

"But Moorely…" I shake my head and take a bite of bell pepper with hummus. "They're senior citizens. They spend their days making brooms from found twigs."

"Aw, sod off, Crawford. They're all still quite sharp. Hell, half of them used to have our jobs teaching here at the college. You know what they're making me do? Foot rubs. Bunion massage. Don't send me in there alone!"

I groan at the thought of spending time with diabetic senior feet. But a bargain is a bargain. If I want my funding proposal to move forward at a realistic pace, I need Abigail to have the proper equipment to help me without her interfering with the settings on my wireless mouse. "Fine. How long to retrieve the file?"

He seems to melt with relief. "Oh, hell. I can get you the information on a flash drive in a few hours. I just need to teach my intro course first."

I return to my office and find myself with free time, as no students have chosen to take advantage of open hours. My thoughts wander back to that article Abigail and her co-workers were reading, and then to her crying softly in my arms last night. If people have always been a mystery to me in general, women have been a whole different level of confusing. The widely-accepted view that they are driven by emotion makes them feel unreachable to me.

Clearly, Heather was not reachable, not for the long term. I had barely considered her while I was in the space station. She was right to leave, I think. Although perhaps she could have chosen a different method of departure.

It seems like common courtesy to give someone advance warning if one plans to dissolve a marriage contract. My mother has said that women don't respond well to being ignored. I find this confusing as well. I go months without speaking to my sister, for instance, and she's still very happy to share her beer in exchange for my input on flavor and consistency. But do we share intimacy, my family and I? Or just history?

After Heather left, I realized I am not capable of partnership because I am not capable of emotional intimacy. I thought maybe I was making headway with Abigail. She seemed grateful for my hug…but not my kiss.

The file of information about Asa Wexler sits on the corner of my desk, reminding me of the growing close connection I have with my tenant. I felt compelled to hug her last night, which is unusual for me. After she told me about her struggles with her former lover, I felt so angry. I enjoy Abigail—she understands me and has such strong communication skills. She is helping me realize my career goals and all she asked in return was help lifting weights. Which I enjoy anyway!

But this article about oral pleasure—it suggests a way to give a woman an orgasm without first connecting to her emotionally. The more I think about it, the more I want to try this with Abigail. I want to make her climax, to see what that looks like.

My pulse has increased rapidly by the time my phone rings. I am grateful for the distraction from my thought spiral. Sara calls to let me know she's made headway negotiating with Heather's attorneys. "Headway is not victory, though, Hunter."

"As I said, I am more than happy to pay her a sum of money. I am not willing to continue a contractual relationship with her that includes future earnings."

"I know, dude. Give me time and patience, ok?"

"I feel no sense of urgency here." Wait. Perhaps that is false. I am still legally married until this is resolved, and suddenly that seems wrong. "Actually, Sara?"

"Yep."

"I don't want to be married to Heather any longer. I am feeling anxious to end that."

"I know, Hunter. She did you dirty, buddy. I'm working on it. Hey, how are things as a landlord? Everything working out ok with Abigail as a tenant?"

"Abigail painted her bedroom. I hadn't considered that the tenant might change the wall colors."

Sara pauses on the other end of the line. "Well, do you want me to add that into the lease for next year? Did she ruin the carpets or something?"

"No." I am not sure why I mentioned the wall color. "She is a very excellent tenant. I think the color she chose in the bedroom is more appropriate for the space."

"Ok, then. Glad that's working out."

"I am fond of Abigail." I am uncertain why I am sharing this information with Sara. I think, actually, that she and her wife Indigo are friendly with Abigail. They helped her move in and lent her the furniture from my father, after all.

"Hunter...I'm glad you like Abigail. She's been through some rough times. I feel like I need to say that Indigo and I are ready to fuck up the next man who hurts her."

"I, too, would want to get violent if someone harms Abigail."

Sara actually laughs, which I'm not sure I've ever heard her do before. "I don't just mean physical harm, Hunter. Anyway, I have a client coming in. I'll talk to you soon." She hangs up before she can elaborate and I'm left to my racing thoughts of Abigail, her emotions, and my strong desire to attempt the Kivin technique to bring her pleasure.

21

Abigail

Diana and Indigo strong-armed me into joining them on the Autumn Apple planning committee. At first I felt like I was back at home—with everyone telling me what to do—but then I realized there's a huge difference between my parents insisting I join the family business and my friends asking for my communication skills for social media and other marketing for the town festival.

And, after all, I do owe Indigo a solid for lending me all the furniture. I keep trying to give it back to her a bit at a time, but she pretends she can't hear me when I offer. So I help her proofread the advertisements she puts in the tourist newsletters when she promotes the Inn.

The main issue in planning the Autumn Apple festival seems to be alcohol. Most everyone wants there to be some, but the people who don't...really don't want there to be alcohol. My outsider perspective is that this town seemed really relieved by Prohibition, and the residents opposed to alcohol sales have had family living in Oak Creek ever since.

I don't think my parents would agree to live in a town where they couldn't buy beer for football games. Where my brothers didn't have easy access to a hockey bar. I snort, momentarily giddy that the town's dry status might act as a barrier keeping my family out of my business for awhile.

Between lifting weights with Hunter, drafting up a funding proposal for Hunter, and Autumn Apple planning sessions with my friends, I haven't had much time to miss my family...or respond to their phone calls.

The girls and I all meet after work at the Inn, where Indigo has a full house and spends our meeting baking scones. She keeps stopping between batches to draw maps directing her guests to Oak Creek's various craft or antique shops.

Diana yanks the pocket door closed to keep people out of the kitchen and plunks a file on the counter, sending up a poof of flour while Indigo rolls out her next batch of baked goods.

"You see, Abigail," Diana says, "Oak Creek is a dry town. The college campus is dry. But the Apple fest simply must include hard apple cider or the people will revolt."

She points to a map of the town limits, a giant red line with angry hash marks drawn around the boundaries where nobody can sell alcohol. Some enterprising businesswoman built a bar directly across the street from the no-booze line, and I've spent a few nights with my friends drinking pints at the Nobler Experiment. "Tessy has a good thing going at her bar, and she will absolutely come at you with a shotgun if you try to sell hooch anywhere near her establishment. And the problem is that she is the county council woman in charge of festival permits."

"So how are you going to sell hard cider?"

Indigo smiles so intently I wonder whether she's heard us or just tasted one of her scones. She says, beaming, "Sara figured it all out! Didn't you, babe? We aren't going to SELL the cider. We're going to *donate* the cider to people who buy apples."

She dances around the kitchen table to kiss Sara on the forehead while Diana talks me through the logistics of what we need.

"The flyers and info for the festival will have to be *very* clear and very specific," she says. "No donations for anyone under 21, etc., etc. Maybe we shouldn't even sell apples to anyone under 21…how will we get that past Hastings?"

"The newspaper guy?"

"He's dryer than an old raisin," Diana says, snatching a warm scone from Indigo's tray. "Fuck, this is amazing. Did you use my rosemary?" Indigo nods as Diana continues. "Hastings runs a smut rag paper of half truths, and yet, he's the leading force for keeping this town dry! He somehow has clout with all the Acorns, even though he's not retired like them, and Ed gets the votes he needs every single time this comes up for discussion."

"Acorns?"

"They're like…mafia is the wrong word. Let's just focus on the newspaper ad for the cider booth and we can talk Acorns over hard liquor sometime."

The next day, I'm too overwhelmed with work and Autumn Apple stuff to even think about lifting weights. I text Hunter from work that I'll come over a bit later to show him what I've got so far on his proposal. He was showing me around his lab last week, all the different tissue samples he wants to study. He comes alive when he talks about science. Instead of the sharp edge and short sentences, he's animated and excited. I can almost feel him vibrating when he talks about the potential that can come from understanding the aging process on human flesh. I'd probably be grossed out if he weren't so excited about it all.

But Hunter is far from gross. He hasn't tried to kiss me again, and every day that I'm sitting in a bag chair in his house, leaning close to him, I get so distracted thinking about his lips.

He makes me feel like helping him write a proposal will help to save the world, like my work with him and with the university really matters for society. I never thought about it that way before, that my ideas about communication can make a real difference for people. Hunter reminds me that my work here is important, not just for the people of this small town, but for all the students who come through the school and all the brilliant ideas they'll think of while they're studying here.

Of course, Hunter doesn't phrase it that way. He uses phrases like "maximum impact" and "fundamental changes to research infrastructure," but I know what he means. And I appreciate him reminding me.

It's nice hanging out with people who are so driven. I guess my dad was driven to create a business. My brothers all seemed just…content to join him.

I want *more*. Everyone in my life seemed to be floating along until I came to Oak Creek. Now I see what "more" could really look like. Rose is away in eastern Europe somewhere having dinner with foreign alumni from the college, asking them to make donations to the endowment to go toward financial aide for students. She's determined to come back with $50 million in pledges. Just from this one dinner!

And Hunter—he literally wants to go past the moon. Talk about motivated. I try not to let myself get too excited about his promise to rescue my novel from my laptop, but just thinking about everyone I've come to know here gets me so excited to work on it again. What if I can really finish it someday? What if, like Hunter, *my* ideas can move people?

My head is still in the clouds later when I wander into Hunter's townhouse. I freeze in my tracks when I notice that he has a real chair at his desk, next to his ergonomic Star Trek chair. "Woah," I say. "You bought furniture?"

Hunter looks up from his monitor and glances at the chair. "Oh." The new addition is a dark red wooden captains chair. "Yes. I'm told it's high quality craftsmanship."

"I can see that," I say. "But what made you double the amount of furniture in your house?"

He shrugs. "It seemed prudent to get you someplace to sit. You should be comfortable while we sit together." He looks at me in that intense way of his, without blinking.

"You bought it just for me?"

He seems to consider this. "You inspired me to purchase it, but I will also invite my family to sit in it if they decide to visit."

It's hard to explain how much it means to me that this specific man did something kind, with me in mind. I can tell it means a lot that he thought of me this way. I sink into the chair, running my hands up and down the smooth arms. "I love it."

I lean over to pat his arm and shiver at the now-familiar electric spark as our skin connects. He doesn't break our gaze, and stares at me with liquid brown eyes. His face is so unreadable. He says, "I have your data."

I blink. "What?"

"Your data. My colleague was able to pull your data from your hard drive."

My heart stops beating for a few minutes and I just stare, open-mouthed. I hadn't really wanted to fully hope that would be possible. I held onto a tiny sliver of maybe, but was steeling myself that my work was gone forever, along with my life in Ohio.

I almost don't know what to make of this news. In the few seconds between heartbeats, my thoughts zoom through possibilities. I can go sit in the coffee shop and work on my novel. *My novel.* "You have it?"

Hunter leans to the side and lifts up a sleek, silver laptop. He hands it to me. "What's this?" I see him grit his teeth as if he's trying to decide what to say. "I mean, I know it's a laptop, Hunter. Is it yours?"

"I bought it for you," he says. He licks his lower lip and I focus on the way it moves above the dark stubble growing in. He must have forgotten to shave today, which means he was really distracted. Upon realizing that I know his habits so well, I gasp. I can't do this. I'm not ready for any kind of relationship. I can't be memorizing a man's grooming habits.

"Hunter, I can't accept this."

"The expense is insignificant for me," he says. "Well, provided my divorce settlement goes as well as Sara predicts."

I snort out a brief laugh. "Did you just make a joke?"

He rubs a palm across his chin, thinking. "I suppose I did," he says.

"Hunter, this laptop…it's too much."

"I could have lied and said it was a refurbishment from the college, but I felt it was important to be truthful," he says.

"Thank you, Hunter. It's just that…things are…I can't get romantically involved with anyone right now."

Another long pause from him. I remind myself that Hunter takes longer than many people to respond, especially if the conversation is about emotions and feelings. I try not to rush him as I wait for him to say something.

Eventually, after an agonizingly long ten seconds, he says, "I can't identify whether I have romantic feelings for you, Abigail. But I am certainly fond of you. And I feel invested in helping you feel happy. I have observed that writing makes you happy."

"You've observed that?"

He nods. "I can see your pulse quicken—the side of your neck ticks when you're writing. And the rise and fall of your chest slows as you think about a sentence, and then I've seen you smile as you type the sentence."

"You noticed all that?"

"Yes." He leans back a bit in his chair, seeming more at ease now. Now it's my turn to pause before I answer him, but he doesn't seem outwardly bothered by a silent gap in our conversation.

I've never met anyone like Hunter before. He's very self-aware, and always totally honest. There's no filter here, and it's refreshing to know exactly where I stand with someone, even if it's agonizing to know that he's been studying me intently to determine whether I'm happy. "I feel a little overwhelmed," I tell him.

I see him swallow. "Have I made a social error again?"

"No, Hunter. I'm just not used to people seeing me."

22

Hunter

Abigail begrudgingly agrees to accept the laptop after I assure her that I've come to think of our time together lifting weights as social time. Her work on my proposal, then, is not being fairly compensated. Hence the laptop.

I enjoy watching her open the new computer. She takes delight in setting up a password, and when I hand her the thumb drive with her file on it, she cradles it as if it were epithelial tissue, so delicate.

I take time to memorize the expression on her face as she opens the file containing the draft of her. novel. I try to scan her entire body, observing her response—I already knew her pulse was elevated and her cheeks were flushed—I contain my desire to wonder aloud what an MRI would show of her brain activity at that moment.

She immediately clutches the computer to her chest and asks if we can go work on my proposal somewhere in public. "Like the bakery or even the library!"

I shake my head. "The library isn't acceptable. I can hear the bag piper from inside the library, and Mary Pat's book club meets at the coffee shop in the afternoons."

Abigail bites her lip. "I keep forgetting to join Mary Pat for that. But, Hunter, I really want to go out somewhere now that I have the ability to be portable."

She grabs my hand and tugs me out the door, nearly running, explaining that she's going to buy me a beer at the Nobler Experiment and we're going to plot there like real business executives. "Doesn't all the magic happen at happy hour? Isn't that a saying?"

"I had not heard this saying before, Abigail."

It doesn't take us long to walk outside town to the entrance of the pub. The atmosphere is crowded and I take a minute in the doorway to asses. It seems like the level of conversation is loud enough to feel like white noise, without an overpowering juke box or performer competing for my attention. "Yes," I say. "We can get work done here."

Abigail has not let go of my hand since she pulled me from my living room, and I take a moment to appreciate how natural, how nice it feels to be touching her affectionately. Tessy stares down at our entwined fingers and Abigail drops my hand to clutch the edge of the bar while she studies the specials. "What's good, Tessy?"

I note that Tessy appears pleased to see Abigail, that people at the bar recognize her and greet her warmly. I can't recall getting this sort of reception going out with Heather. Even Heather's friends always seemed firm lipped and stiff. Like nobody was ever at ease.

I enjoy the warm closeness of Abigail when she slides in next to me in the booth, making sure our pint glasses are placed far from her new computer. "I think I feel ready to bang out the project narrative, Hunter," she says. I watch as her fingers fly over the keyboard. I marvel at how Abigail gives shape to the importance of my research. She puts into words exactly why I believe someone should take a chance and fund this work. I can only watch her in awe.

"You've unlocked my ideas," I say.

She grins, and I love thinking I put that smile on her face. "I just listened really hard to what you weren't saying," she says.

The day after we complete a rough draft of the proposal, Abigail tells me she's too busy with my mother and with Autumn Apple work to come over and work out.

I find that my afternoons feel emptier without her, without the anticipation of sitting beside her to talk. Loneliness is not a familiar experience for me.

I'm not entirely sure that's what I'm experiencing, but I find I am unable to sit alone at home anymore. I walk through town toward my brother's office. Is this restlessness?

Archer works as a CPA, but is generally accepted as the mayor of Oak Creek. Our town holds no such office—we are governed by a town council, and Archer is certainly not part of that group, but even the council comes to him for advice.

Perhaps he should have considered a degree in psychology like our mother. Or perhaps he's content the way things are. When I arrive at his office he's blaring country music, leaning close to his work station where he has spreadsheets up on two large computer monitors.

I wait for him to notice me, and when he doesn't, I walk around his desk and set my hand on his shoulder. My father has always said it's polite to cough as a way to announce your presence in a room, but with the music so loud I felt I needed another approach. My touch seems to startle Archer, who leaps from his chair and punches me in the shoulder.

Not expecting that, I fall backward, with him on top of me. "Jesus Christ, Hunter," he shouts. He climbs off me and turns off the music at his desk. "You scared the shit out of me."

"You really should lock your office door if you're going to play music *and* become deeply engrossed in your work," I say, rising to my feet.

He shakes his head. "What are you doing here in the middle of the day?"

I look at my watch to confirm and remind him that it's after 4pm. "Shit," he says, saving his work. He looks around his office at the afternoon light coming through the window. "What's up?"

"I had come to ask a favor, but now I feel that you owe me something to make up for punching me."

"How about we're even since I drove to fucking Texas to get you and let you stay at my house."

"You said that was a kindness I didn't need to repay."

Archer rolls his eyes at me. "What do you need, Hunter?"

I can't tell if he's actually frustrated or just exasperated, but I press on. "I would like you to come play cards with me and a colleague Friday night."

"That's the favor? Hanging out with you?"

I consider leaving out the rest of the pertinent information, but decide it's better to be fully honest. "And the Acorns as well."

"Aw, shit, Hunter. Those fucking guys. They're going to make you talk about Heather, you know."

"I'm prepared for that," I tell him. I put my hands in my pockets and wait for his response. He often tries to use silence as a tactic to get people to relent in an argument, but I am unbothered by silence.

He sighs. "Fine. I'll drive. Pick you up at 7?"

I shake my head. "They start early. Best to make it 6."

The rest of the week, it takes all of my concentration to interact with my students. As we approach mid-term exams, they all begin to exhibit stress responses, despite my explanations and suggestions for study techniques. I even tried to play a guided meditation on calm in class one day, but this just resulted in giggles and fidgeting sounds. My mother sternly reminded me that I cannot raise my voice to the students, even when exasperated. So I spend an entire class period on Friday tediously reviewing all the parts of the cell and each of their functions.

By the time I've re-explained mitochondria a third time, I run my fingers through my hair, tell them, falsely, that they've made progress, and dismiss class early. This level of frustration is unusual for me.

On Friday, my restlessness persists even after an intense workout with added jump rope sessions. My brother is due to arrive in an hour, and I feel as though a chemical reaction is detonating inside my body. I make myself a glass of chocolate milk and sit at my computer, which only reminds me that Abigail is not sitting in her new chair as she should be. *Abigail.*

Bringing up her name causes a pulse in whatever emotion simmers beneath the surface of my skin. I don't like this sensation, and I like it even less when I realize I've gotten another erection. I stare down at my cock as if it were a foreign body part. Then I start to think about how long it's been since I've *used* my dick for anything. How many months has it been? Perhaps the answer to the buzzing sensation filling my body is release.

I waste no time pulling my shaft from my athletic shorts. I sit back in my desk chair, stroking myself, and my thoughts shift immediately to Abigail. I feel better already, and decide this is just what I need to calm the vibrations in my veins.

I envision the pulse in her neck ticking just above the heaving swell of her bosom. I imagine what it would look like if she were lying on the ground beneath me. I stroke myself faster as I think about the shape of her ass when I stand behind her, the feel of her soft skin when I touch her back.

If I close my eyes, I can smell her scent wafting over me the time I sat on her bed.

I remember that I have photographs of her in my phone.

Fumbling around, I pull up the image of her bent over, gripping the barbell. *Yes, there.* I can see her nipples pebbled through her tank top.

I can tell I am close to erupting as I stare at her. She bites her lip in the photo and I image what she would look like if her hand was gripped around my cock instead of the barbell.

I imagine what it would feel like to gently rub my thumbs across those thick nubs of nipple, to feel them rise at my touch. I remember the soft groans she makes when she's straining herself lifting weights and pretend that it's me causing those sounds. That it's me bringing her pleasure.

I groan and reach for the towel I had thrown on my desk after my workout. My wrist flicks up and down my cock quickly now, and I know I'm on the verge. Just as I'm about to explode, I see the back door open, and there she is.

There is Abigail herself standing in my doorway.

The sight of her sends me over the edge and with one final flick, I am emptying myself into the towel, pulsing into my fist, moaning in complete ecstasy.

23

Abigail

I know I shouldn't have accepted the laptop from Hunter, but it's already improved my life dramatically. I had been sketching out ideas by hand for Sara and Indigo to type up for marketing materials for Autumn Apple. Now that I can type my own thoughts at my own pace, I've completed absolutely everything on our checklist and even set up a website for the event.

Every evening, I've been teaching myself to use content management software, which is so thrilling because now I can also help Rose with updates to the college website and share her fundraising successes more quickly. It's funny how one little thing like a laptop can make such a difference, but I guess it's not just the laptop. I have the freedom to use my skills, to stretch my ideas. I have people here who get excited about change.

Well. Some changes. Ed Hastings tapped me on the shoulder when I was working at the coffee shop the other day, wanting to "make sure" I wasn't planning to skirt the rules about alcohol in his dry town. I bought him a muffin, and that seemed to appease him for a bit. Mary Pat told me he's planning to write a big story about how I refuse to cooperate with town rules. I got Ed to tell me about his background as a journalist and it seemed to make him happy to hear that I aspire to be a great writer like him.

Rose told me to go ahead and work from home this week, since she's going to Panama to speak at some conference, and I've been finishing up my work day by 3, using the afternoons to chip away at my novel. Has it only been a week since Hunter gave me this computer? My whole life has changed again, it seems like.

Friday, I decide to hang around the house, doing laundry and sipping tea in the kitchen while I write from a stool at the counter instead of the coffee shop or the library.

When I hear the familiar sound of Hunter grunting and groaning, I realize it's been days since I've made time to exercise.

Then I feel guilty, because I haven't been working with him on his proposal, either. Life has been such a whirlwind. If I'm really honest, I've been avoiding him a bit until I figure out my feelings since he bought me the chair and the laptop. There's no denying each of those gifts bring up intense emotions. We had such a nice time working together at the pub, even held hands walking there. I don't know what to make of it all. I'm definitely attracted to him, but I'm in no position to start a relationship when I can't even figure out what my life plan should be.

Things just feel so right with Hunter, though. He's brutally honest, up front, and completely earnest at all times. He's passionate about his work and even though he lost his job, he maintained his staunch belief that his research matters. He refuses to stop doing the work, even if he's no longer being paid for it. I find that passion so...sexy. I find it sexy.

Everything about Hunter Crawford is sexy, from his intense stares to his taut ass to the way he touched my face when he tried to kiss me in my bedroom. And then my stupid body reacted and he left my house thinking I didn't want him.

So when I hear Hunter grunt again through the thin walls of the kitchen, I decide to go on over and join him. It'll feel good to lift weights with him. To be near him.

Only, when I open the back door to his place, he's not lifting weights.

I freeze in my tracks inside his doorway as I see his hand flying at his crotch and realize I have, once again, made a terrible assumption about the noises coming from Hunter Crawford's house.

"I'm so, so sorry," I say, backing up as he moans. "Oh my god, I'm leaving. I'm so sorry."

"Abigail, wait." His voice is oddly calm, and his body seems relaxed in a way I've not seen before.

"I...should let you have privacy," I say, but I don't leave. I'm transfixed, staring at his crotch as he tucks his cock back in his shorts.

"I was thinking about you," he says, his voice like liquid sex. "And then you appeared."

I bite my lip, unsure what to make of this. Was he really thinking of me while he did *that?*

"Do you remember that article you were reading with your colleagues?" Hunter tosses a towel on the floor and stands, walking over to me. His hair is disheveled and I see his athletic shorts bulge. He's still at least semi hard, even after he came.

I nod. Of course I remember that article. I keep dreaming about it at night and waking up when I realize it's Hunter crouched beside my body, worshipping me in my dreams.

He stands so close to me, but doesn't touch me. I breathe through my nose, trying to calm my racing thoughts, my soaring pulse. This feels too real, too big, and then he speaks again. "I'd like to kiss you if that's all right."

I nod, barely, but then I'm lost because he has pulled me against his body, devouring my mouth, claiming me with his tongue. He moans into my mouth and I'm ruined for all other kisses.

I can feel his heart beat against my chest as I open for him. My hands sink into his dark hair, slide to his sweaty shoulders. I inhale the salty, musky scent of him, so raw, so feral, and I groan. I want him, very badly.

"Abigail," he whispers against my lips. "This is exactly what I imagined it would be like," he says as he licks the delicate skin of my throat. I drop my head back and he nips at my flesh. I love this side of him, crazed with passion. My blood boils in my veins as his hands travel up and down my sides, as his fingers squeeze into my ass.

"Hunter," I breathe. "Yes." I suck on his bottom lip, pressing my body against his, rocking my hips against his cock, desperate for friction. Desperate for release.

"I want to pleasure you, Abigail," he says, and when I nod, I feel him yank down my leggings and panties in one strong tug. With my pants halfway to my knees I wobble, and Hunter lowers us both to the padded mat he has covering the floor in his dining room, next to the weight bench. And I don't even care that I'm going at it on the floor. All I can feel are his hands on my skin, traveling up and down my legs as he removes my leggings, leaving me bare.

He licks my thighs as he settles beside me, just like the illustration in the article. Just like in my dream. He raises his dark head to make eye contact with me and gently nudges my legs apart with his hands. I place a hand on his neck, breathing heavily. "Yes, Hunter. Please."

When his strong hands make contact with my clit, I scream. He parts my delicate folds with the fingers of one hand, stroking my slit with the other, then sliding a fingertip inside my body. "Abigail. You. Are. So. Wet." He punctuates each word with a stroke of his long, hot fingers and my hips buck against his body. My heels dig into the floor and my knees fall open even farther.

Then he dips his head and begins to lick. I can hear myself moaning, feel myself thrashing on the ground. This is unlike anything I have ever felt before. Hunter Crawford has unlocked the secret to my body and swallowed the key along with every drop of my excitement. "Oooh, yes. Hunter, fuck. Yes. God, just like that."

His tongue laps sideways across my clit as he kneels to the right of my body. His left hand parts my folds and works at my clit, and then his right hand begins to massage me inside and out. He slips a long finger gently along my opening, gently working toward my ass.

"Hmmm," he moans against my body, and then sucks my clit between his teeth.

All conscious thought leaves me as I detonate. I feel his finger thrust inside my center and my body pulses, contracts, spasming. I feel my limbs thrashing as I scream his name, coming so hard I see stars and gasp for breath.

Never have I come to orgasm so quickly with a partner, but then, never have I been with someone who pays such careful attention. As I return to earth and open my eyes, I find Hunter staring at me, smiling, caressing me so gently. Aftershocks of my orgasm jolt through me, and Hunter keeps his hands on me, smiling at me, until the spasms stop. I feel completely safe and content. Boneless, utterly at peace.

This feeling vanishes when I hear the front door open and a man's voice curse. "Aw Jesus fuck, Hunter. Shit. I'll wait in the car."

24

Hunter

Archer showed up at my house seventeen minutes early. I don't understand why he would do this.

After he closes the front door I look down at Abigail, spread open before me on the ground. Her creamy white skin is fully exposed, just for me. It takes all my effort not to dive back in and continue to ravish her, perhaps switch sides to see if I can make her climax again from the opposite direction. What would it be like, I wonder, to use my dominant hand at her clit while my left moved in and out of her body?

I shake these thoughts away. Much as I'd like to, I cannot spend the evening massaging the beautiful skin of Abigail Baker. I made a commitment to play cards with Moorely and my brother. I cough. "Abigail," I say, reaching for her clothes. "I apologize for the intrusion. I have an appointment with my brother this evening."

She sits up, and her demeanor seems guarded. Her body seems closed to me, suddenly. "Oh," she says.

"I have 16 minutes to shower and change before I have to meet Archer in the driveway," I tell her. I begin to lift her to her feet. When she seems a bit unsteady, I help her step into her leggings. I can sense that I am making an error in etiquette, but I also know it's wrong to cancel plans with my brother. This interlude with Abigail was, after all, unplanned.

"Ok," she says. And then the silence between us feels...heated. Different than usual. Something is off.

She bites her lip. I see tears well up in her eyes. This isn't good. "I very much enjoyed our experience together," I tell her. She nods. "I made a prior commitment with my brother, not knowing you and I would try the Kivin method of oral sex."

"Yes," she says, tugging up her pants. "Of course. I should have called before I came over." And she walks out of the house without a further word.

When she leaves, I can tell that she's not being fully honest. She is unsettled. But I don't have time to figure out what to do about that because my brother is waiting.

I hurry through my shower and step outside into Archer's truck with one minute to spare. "You were early," I say by way of greeting.

He shakes his head and starts driving. "When were you going to tell me you're fucking Abigail?"

The Nerd and the Neighbor

When I don't answer right away he punches me in the thigh. "Ouch! I was thinking, Archer. I was trying to decide if oral sex counts as 'fucking,' in which case the answer is that I've only been fucking her for approximately 20 minutes."

He pulls the truck over to the side of the road abruptly. "Wait. I walked in on your first time with her and you just left with me?"

"Yes." This is seeming less and less like the appropriate course of action, which is upsetting and confusing because Archer and I have a commitment with Moorely.

"Hunter, Jesus. You have to call her."

"Hmm." I look at my phone in the console of Archer's truck.

"You gotta text her at least. *Sweet dreams, I'll be dreaming of you. Can't wait to see you tomorrow.* That sort of thing. This is serious, Hunter. Don't fuck this up."

"Those are uncharacteristic things for me to say."

Archer starts driving again and almost hits me, but retracts his hand. "Do you like this woman?"

"I am quite fond Abigail. Absolutely."

"Ok, then plan out what you're going to write and do not hit send until I say it's ok."

We pull into the parking lot of the Acorns' club house before I can come up with anything that seems appropriate to send to my next-door neighbor who caught me masturbating and then let me massage her vulva. "I can't think of anything apart from 'I'd very much like to do that again soon.'"

"Oh my god, Hunter." Archer kicks open the door and Moorely, who looks sweaty already, stands up from the table and rushes over to us.

"Good on you, mate. Thank you, truly, for helping me out here."

"Moorely, this is my brother Archer."

"Cheers," he says, while Archer simultaneously says, "You wanna hear what my dumbass brother just did?"

To my horror, the 3 of us sit down at a table full of senior citizens as Archer talks about my personal life. The cards seem forgotten, hearing aids are adjusted. They all listen to my brother, rapt, as he describes my Pandora's box. I cover my face with my hands when Archer tells them he thinks I am the world's biggest moron. And then they collectively try to work out how I should proceed with Abigail.

Don, who taught in the OCC creative writing department for 30 years, suggests I send her a link to a love poem.

Lamar, whom I think I replaced in biology, suggests having Diana drop off flowers immediately.

Christian the retired anthropologist just laughs, until Archer gives more details on what he saw.

I am not embarrassed—that's not an emotion I typically experience—but I am defensive that Archer would share these details. I want to keep my experience with Abigail private. Something just for us. Something that's mine alone.

The men are fascinated, though, and the discussion quickly shifts to the difficulty of successful oral sex and the elusive female orgasm. Moorely even pulls up the article on his phone and reads it aloud.

Soon, they all begin asking me for pointers until I feel my skin crawling with discomfort. Lamar slaps the table and declares, "I'm goin' home to try this out with

Mary Pat," which draws peals of laughter from everyone else. I start to relax a bit, certain the Acorns will be less strict if they're in a good mood. They tend to insist we ante up with non-cash items like help with yard work or rides to the podiatrist. Before my last trip to the space station, I came home to Oak Creek for a visit and found myself giving insulin injections to some of the Acorns while they watched *The Price is Right.*

Thankfully, Moorely redirects everyone to the card game while I tap out a message to Abigail.

I'm very glad I finally kissed you. I think about you frequently. I hope we will see each other tomorrow.

When Archer drops me off after cards, I see that Abigail's lights are still on downstairs. I don't want to frighten her and try to peek around the curtains, but I have to see her again. Immediately. I can almost still taste her, the heady and powerful taste of her arousal. For *me.*

After I sent the text, I had imagined she would come over to my house tomorrow evening like usual. I planned to swoop in and kiss her again then, but now that I realize she is still awake, sitting this close to me, I find I cannot move my thoughts from her. I can almost smell the rosemary in her hair and lavender on her skin.

I tap softly on her front door.

Soon after, I see her eye appear by the curtain, pupil contracted in concern. Then I feel relief when her face softens and she cracks the door open.

"Abigail," I say softly, not entirely certain why I'm whispering. "May I come in?"

She doesn't say anything but opens the door, so I step into her house. I have always had a sensitivity to smell. New places overwhelm me. I could only stand the space station because it smelled so sterile, so constantly of motor oil and cleaning solution.

But Abigail's house smells like a meadow, like sunshine and wild plants. She stands leaning against the wall, hands in the pockets of her sweatpants, biting her lip. "I wasn't sure what to make of…what happened," she says. She never did respond to my text.

"I feel very conflicted about my departure, Abigail. I made a commitment to my brother, and I— well I have a lot of experience overlooking my commitments to people when I get engrossed in my work. It's not something I'm proud of." I start rambling to her, telling her all the things Heather used to scream at me in the night when I'd stagger in from the lab, feeling triumphant, only to find her crying and throwing wasted theater tickets in my face or dumping ruined food in the garbage.

I sigh. "So, I hope you can understand that it felt important to me to—"

And then Abigail's arms are around my neck and she's kissing me. I quickly scan my body to verify I'm not hallucinating. I feel her soft curves pressing against me, my thickening erection pulsing against her stomach. I moan against her mouth and I feel her smile.

"I like it when you come unhinged," she says. "I think about you frequently, too."

She startles me by shoving me back against the opposite wall of the hallway. "Thank you for telling me why it mattered so much that you keep your promise to your brother," she says, punctuating her words with small kisses against my jawline.

"Abigail, this is all very unexpected."

She sucks on the skin at the base of my neck, drawing out another involuntary groan. She pulls back and asks, "unexpected is not unwanted, right?"

"Oh, Abigail." I grip her shoulders and meet her eyes. "Make no mistake. I want you."

25

Abigail

I love seeing this side of Hunter, this raw, passionate, wild energy, all of it still laser-focused on me. I definitely felt rejected when he took off earlier, but knowing how hard he works just on talking to people, I feel really grateful for his explanation of why it was important to keep his plans with his brother.

And holy wow. This payoff is worth it. Hunter stalks me like prey, nipping his teeth into me, massaging me everywhere I didn't know I needed it. He seems concentrated on bringing me pleasure as he lifts me off the ground and thrusts his hips against my center. I feel friction where I need it most and I moan into his mouth as I wrap my legs around his back.

Hunter pulls back and looks around, as if he's considering tossing me on the ground again. "Take me upstairs," I tell him. I want this experience to last longer than this afternoon, and my hardwood floors aren't comfortable.

He grunts in response, digging his fingers into my thighs as he carries me upstairs. I try to fumble for the lights as he walks past the switch, but I miss and I don't want to stop trying to remove his shirt.

Fumbling in the dark by memory, he trips on my shoes and we both land on the edge of my bed. I can just stretch and reach the lamp. Hunter slides to his knees on the carpet in front of me and begins to strip me again, only this time he focuses on my top half. I sit on the edge of the mattress while he lifts off my shirt and then palms my breasts.

He ducks his dark head to first one, then the other nipple. He sucks each one slowly, hard, swirling his tongue around each peak until I cry out while his fingers work magic on the other breast. Each time he rasps his flat tongue over one of my nipples, I feel the jolt straight through my body, as if he's found a chord connecting his mouth to the pleasure center of my brain.

He moans again as I finally wrestle his shirt over his head, breaking his connection with my skin just long enough to toss the cotton across the room. I pull his hot, naked torso against mine, reveling in the hard strength of him against me. "Hunter," I breathe. "I want you to lie on top of me."

I want to feel the long weight of him pressing against my whole body, to sink beneath him in the mattress while he does more magical things to my body with his tongue. It's as if all the years studying the behavior of cells taught him exactly how to service mine, and as Hunter slides my pajama pants down I quiver with anticipation.

I can still feel echoes of his earlier work, my clit throbbing with need as his hands massage my legs. He murmurs against my skin, dotting kisses along my legs while he talks about—"Wait, what did you say?"

He raises his head, rests his chin against my thigh as he strokes my leg. "I said I want to study your vasculature."

I don't mean to laugh when he's looking at me so intently, but I can't help it. "Nobody has ever said anything like that to me during sex," I say, running my fingers through his hair.

By way of response, he rises to his knees and slides his jeans and boxers down his slim hips. My eyes are drawn to the dark thatch of hair beneath the hard lines of his abs, and then to the thick length of his shaft. Hunter begins to stroke himself, still staring at me. "I have a condom in my wallet," he says.

"Good," I tell him, breathless.

Finding his jeans, he starts to fumble in the back pocket, procuring a shiny foil packet. I bite my lip in anticipation, anxious. At last, Hunter sets the packet on the pillow and eases me up higher on the bed. Naked, we lie together and the room is so quiet I can hear both of us breathing. He says, "if we lie still together long enough, our heart rates would synchronize."

"I don't want to lie still," I pant into his ear, thrusting my hips up against him. I love the warm heat of his cock pressed against my body. I nudge my thighs wider and he settles between my legs.

I meet his eyes then and I sense that he feels worried, too. "What's up?" I ask.

"I...haven't done this for some time."

"Oh. Well. Me neither."

"I'm still technically married. I feel it's important for me to clarify that in case—"

"Hunter, it's ok." I reach between us and he hisses as I wrap my hand around him. "Is this ok?"

"Oh, Abigail. Yes." Hunter closes his eyes, moaning. His hips begin to move as I stroke him. "You feel so good," he says, sucking on the skin on my neck, moving lower to lap at my nipples again.

Squirming a bit to free my arm from our tangle of limbs, I reach for the condom as Hunter begins to rub my clit with his thumb. Again, he has found the perfect rhythm to drive me quickly toward the cliff of release. I can feel my body contracting, pulsing beneath him. I open my eyes to find him staring intently at my face.

I let go of his cock to open the wrapper, drawing another groan from Hunter. He adjusts his weight as I slide the condom on and then he cups my chin, his thumb stroking my jaw delicately. "Are you sure?"

"Yes. Definitely."

And then he slides inside me. I'm so slick with wanting him, it almost eliminates the sting I feel. My body is out of practice. I shudder and Hunter stills. "Abigail," he whispers. "Show me what you need."

I nod, catching my breath, adjusting to the feel of him. Remembering how eager he's been to bring me pleasure, I slowly rock my body against his. My hips tilt and soon I'm controlling the pace. Hunter balances his weight on his forearms, let's me lead, seeming to study me as I slide up and down his cock from beneath.

I realize I have never been the one to set the pace, lead the movement. The power of this control makes me giddy and I start moving faster, harder. I sink my hands into the firm globes of Hunter's ass, bury my tongue in his mouth and begin to thrust with all my power. "I want to be on top," I tell him, and we start to roll.

Seated on top of him, I place my hands on his chest. I swirl my hips and he moans, his eyes beginning to roll up into his head. Hunter reaches up to cup my swaying breasts as I move faster. "Jesus, Hunter, this feels fucking amazing."

For a minute, or maybe it's an hour, I ride him, faster, harder, until his breath comes in grunts and moans. I feel his cock swell inside me. I see him straining his neck, and I know he's close. I want to come together with him, but I just can't— "Touch me," I groan. "Fuck, yes. Hunter, touch me just like that."

His hand is back, sliding between our joined bodies, circling outside my clit, rubbing, then flicking it until we both gasp. I feel the swell of my orgasm build sharply and then I'm crashing down on to him, collapsing on his chest as my body contorts, riding out the waves while he cries my name and buries his fingers in my hair.

Sated, exhausted, panting, I roll off him and curl up against his side. He drops an arm around my shoulder briefly, playing his fingers up and down my arm, but then he suddenly stands. He starts to walk across the room.

My thoughts crash back to earlier when his brother interrupted us, and he just left. Ushered me out the back door, as if making me come was an item on his research checklist and, having completed it, he was immediately on to the next task. Damned if I'm going to let him do that twice in one day.

"What the fuck, Hunter?"

26

Hunter

I freeze in my tracks as Abigail curses at me. I turn slowly, in the process of removing the condom. She stares at the mess in my hand and I sense that once again I have made a foible.

"Are you fucking leaving?" she seems very clear that I should not, so I sit back down on the bed.

"I had planned to go into the bathroom and wipe off," I tell her. "But I can wait if it makes you more comfortable."

Her face softens. "Oh." I see tears well up in her eyes and I grind my teeth, searching my memories for a comparable situation and the proper response.

"I should have told you that's where I was going," I say. "I realize now you are still upset about how I abruptly left earlier this evening."

I see her shoulders sink a bit in relief and know that I'm on the right track with this line of honesty. "I would reach out for you and comfort you," I say, "except that I have semen on my hands from removing the condom."

Abigail snorts in laughter. I feel better, like I can perhaps salvage this evening successfully. "Go on and wash up," she says. "And then come back to me."

After I wash my hands and return to the bedroom, I see she's crawled beneath the covers, folded down one side. I hesitate. *Are we going to sleep? Are we going to rest and then have sex again?* I clear my throat and announce, "Archer only put one condom in my wallet."

"I don't want to talk about your brother, Hunter. Come and hold me, would you?"

I slide into bed beside Abigail, reveling in the strangeness of her wanting to press her body close to mine. And my enjoying this sensation. "To clarify," I start, "would you like me to stay here all night?"

"I would, yes." Abigail takes my hand and rubs her thumb along my knuckles. It feels so nice. So intimate.

She reaches to turn off the light and soon, her breathing slows. I drape my arm over her side and, given this unhindered access and express permission to touch her, I study her in the moonlight. I let my fingers learn the rise and fall of her chest with her breath, the shape of her curves.

I think back on our experience together, how I seemed driven by instinct I did not know I possessed. Everything we did tonight was foreign to me, and yet it felt so familiar. As if I were somehow constructed just to please Abigail.

"I can hear you thinking," she says, rolling over to face me in the bed.

"You can?"

Abigail smiles. I like when she smiles—I don't feel as though she is making fun of me, but rather that she is delighted by the things I say. "I can't actually hear your thoughts, Hunter, but I can sense that your mind is working overtime."

"How can you sense it? What are the signs?"

"I know you want to analyze this stuff and store it away in that brain of yours to use as a datapoint for future human interactions," she says, tracing a finger around my chest in a way that brings attention directly to my hardening cock. "But Hunter, I'm in a post-orgasmic coma right now and I just can't."

"Hmm," I decide to run my fingers through her hair. It's long and dark and full, and it always smells like hair. I'm used to women who pile on products until the layers of scent overpower my thoughts. "I was thinking," I tell her. "It seemed like I was able to...please you..."

"Definitely."

"Well I could feel it. I could feel your body responding to me." She opens her eyes to meet mine as I lift her hand and kiss her knuckles. I had no idea the knuckle had so many nerve endings until Abigail started stroking mine earlier. "I've been lying here thinking about how easily I interpreted your cues. And how good that felt."

"You made me feel so damn good, Hunter."

A long time passes as my mind continues to race. "I wasn't a very good husband, Abigail. But I would very much like to be a good partner for you. If you are interested in that."

I wake up ready to have sex again, but we still don't have another condom. My instinct is to get out of bed and walk to the drug store to get some, but I realize if Abigail wakes while I'm gone or in the process of leaving she will not know how to interpret those actions. I decide to just stare at her while she's sleeping, her face caught in a light smile.

I feel like I've waited my entire life to figure out what it means to desire someone like this, to feel the connection that my parents speak of. When Abigail and I were together last night, I felt like I was pouring a bit of my soul into her along with my release. I am a different person today than yesterday, if that seems possible. I never had this with Heather. I see now that I should not have married her, that comfort and familiarity are no replacement for real connection with another person.

At the same time, I realize that Heather could not have felt real connection with me, either. Knowing she stayed with me for convenience...or profit or fame...eases the sting of regret that has been growing the more I realize I was not a good husband to her.

"Your thoughts are busy again." Abigail wakes and kisses me softly.

"I was trying to decide how to go to the drug store without upsetting you."

"Maybe we should go on our way back from the coffee shop." Abigail's words drift off as I rock my hips against her involuntarily. My blood races as we kiss for a few minutes before Abigail pulls back. "We better go before things get desperate."

She climbs out of bed and begins to dress, bending to get a pair of pants from her bottom drawer. "Abigail, I need to inform you that things will always be desperate, as you say, when it comes to you."

She looks at me over her shoulder, still bent over, and I can feel my erection pulsing against my stomach. "Really?"

I nod. "I've been having impure thoughts about your backside. And your breasts." She laughs and throws my jeans at me.

Walking through town with her feels nice. Familiar and not overwhelming. I don't need down time to rest after spending so much time around her, because I don't seem to need to work as hard to figure out how to interact with her. As long as I verbalize my thoughts, Abigail seems very content, even to enjoy spending time with me.

I find I don't want to keep my hands off of her, and I let my fingers trail up and down her back, stroke through her hair while we wait in line for coffee for Abigail. The barista's gaze lingers on us, and I know there will soon be an article about us in the *Oak Creek Gazette*, but I don't mind. Let them speculate. Let the newspaper brag that Hunter Crawford is romantically involved with Abigail Baker.

We spend the morning together making use of our drug store purchases until my body feels chafed and exhausted. I confess to feeling some relief when she tells me she has to meet with the Autumn Apple committee and I retreat to my lab on campus. Alone with my slides and my computational algorithms, I lose myself to the closest thing I've ever found to meditation. I experience utter clarity and laser focus. A series of orgasms has certainly relieved any buzzing restlessness I was experiencing. By the time I emerge from my data, it's growing dark.

27

Abigail

Indigo, Sara and Diana have spread out on the dining room table of the Inn while some of the guests gather around looking over their shoulders. A retired couple I recognize from before is holding one of the flyers, munching on Indigo's homemade biscuits and commenting that they'll have to book a return visit for the festival.

I trip over someone's duffel bag as I enter the room and everyone turns their head to identify the noise. Kicking the bag to the side, I make my way to the table and they're all still staring at me. "What?" I start smoothing my hair, wondering if I have something on my face.

Diana raises an eyebrow and points her pen at me. "You got fucked last night."

The retired couple titters with laughter and the wife claps me on the back. "That's what I was thinking, too, dear. Looks like you had a good time. George, look at her blush."

Indigo squeals and claps her hands. "This all can wait. I want details. First thing: what was your orgasm tally? This is very important."

Sara rolls her eyes and my jaw works up and down as I try to figure out what to say.

"Oh, lord. You slept with my brother." Diana reaches for a biscuit and, tilting her head, asks, "Was it awful?"

Sara shakes her head. "She doesn't look like it was awful."

"Well good day to all of you," I say, sinking into a chair and wishing it would fall into the abyss. I close my eyes for a minute and then say to each of them, "the tally is 5; it was your brother; it was amazing."

Indigo shoves the pile of papers into a folder as the retired couple leans front on their elbows. "I think we can go ahead and green light all this, Sar," she says. "We've got more important things to discuss."

I finish answering their questions as briefly as they'll allow, and Mabel and George weigh in that it sounds like I've got a good thing going here. I like the sound of that.

"You're glowing, babe," Indigo says, draping an arm around Sara's shoulders. "This is great. Who knew Hunter had it in him?"

Diana pulls up the oral sex article from Cosmo and squints while she starts to read it aloud. "This is kind of amazing," she says. "Sara, come see how this article uses really inclusive language. It's not heteronormative at all. I'm going to try really hard not to think about my brother doing this shit and be happy that you—my friend and a person with a clitoris—got someone to do this for you."

George makes eyes at Mabel and asks Indigo how much time they have before checkout.

Eager to change the topic, I ask Indigo what comes next for the festival. We are two weeks out and I feel like I have no idea what will happen. "Oh, don't worry about that," she says. "The hard part was finishing all this signage. Everyone will just show up next Friday to do their same old job. Did Rose say you could take off Friday to help set up?"

I frown. Rose has a lot going on right now, meeting with alumni like George and Mabel to hit them up for cash. As soon as she got back from Panama, she got some foreign alum staying at their house in the Meadow room, which evidently used to be Fletcher's. "As long as I can get talking points on her desk by that Thursday I think we will be good."

Autumn Apple always gets a lot of involvement from the college students, apparently, looking for something different to do on a weekend. Oak Creek College might excel in academics, but the small town setting doesn't offer much in the way of entertainment. Sara fills me in on all the telltale signs to watch for with the students trying to pass off fake IDs to get hard cider.

The four of us spend the entire day sorting volunteer packets for next weekend and talking about Sara and Indigo's plans to maybe have a baby, which is a whole production apparently for same-sex couples.

Diana's dad calls mid-afternoon to insist she come over for dinner, and I hear him holler through the phone, "Are you there with Hunter's lady-friend? Tell Abigail to come, too."

"I guess you're coming home with me for Dinner with Daniel," she says.

We walk to the Crawford house, where I can smell garlic from half a block away. "Come on inside," Rose sings from the kitchen. She's dancing around with a glass of wine as Daniel bastes a roasting chicken. "The alumni have taken a bus tour to New York City. It's just us tonight. Oh, Abigail, there you are, dear. Listen, next time I really would prefer if you and Hunter can tip us off before we read about your personal activities in the *Gazette*." Rose slides me a glass of wine along with today's "special edition" newspaper.

GROUCHY SCIENTIST WOOS SPEECHWRITER, the headline screams.

"Drink your wine before you read, dear," Rose says. "It'll help."

"Diana, have you heard from your brothers?" Daniel starts rapidly chopping herbs for a sauce that smells amazing.

She shakes her head and stage whispers to me, "This is a family strategy meeting, if you couldn't tell."

Archer strides into the kitchen and kisses his mother on the cheek. "What's up? I got the SOS text."

I start reading the article, which makes it sound like Hunter and I were caught having sex in the middle of Main Street. "Are drug store employees allowed to share information about what people buy??"

"The wine, Abigail," Rose says. "Drink the wine. Archer, I'm sure you've heard by now. We need to decide how we will respond."

"He knew," I blurt to Rose, chugging the wine as she refills my glass. "Archer knew last night!"

"Aw, come on, Abigail. I thought we were friends."

Rose starts scolding him, swatting his upper arm as she yells at him for not giving her and Daniel a heads up that Hunter had a lady-friend. I continue reading about so-called public displays of affection—"Hunter gave me *one* peck on the cheek at the coffee shop!"—but then the article takes a nasty turn I wasn't expecting.

I don't know much about the details of Hunter's separation with his wife, just that she left him and is asking for a lot of money in their divorce. This article suggests that Hunter is somehow creating this relationship with me publicly to manipulate public opinion about his divorce. "We have to wonder what the estranged Mrs. Crawford thinks about another woman glowing with satisfaction from a night spent making love with her spacey spouse." I almost can't get the words out. "What is this, Rose? Does Hunter still talk to Heather?"

Hunter arrives then, seemingly unaware of what's been going on. Diana hands him a beer and nudges him to sit next to me. I slide him the paper and watch his face, trying to gauge his reaction. I feel relief when I see him frown and grit his teeth as he gets toward the end of the article. He throws the paper on the table and turns toward me. "Abigail," he says. "There is no reason for you to think Heather is a consideration for me at all. Please tell me you are not swayed by this inflammatory tirade?"

I shake my head, but the truth is I'm rattled by the article. There are small grains of truth in Ed Hastings' suggestion that I ran out on my old life and haven't looked back. He says I am burying myself into this town's traditions and this town's men, apparently, to escape my demons. Why shouldn't it be a little true that Hunter is just using me strategically? Divorcing Heather will cost him millions at this point.

Daniel plunks a laptop on the table and I look up to see a video chat with a man who looks like Hunter but Rose's blue eyes. He's seated outside somewhere with palm trees in the background. "What's all this about?" the face squints around the room.

"Fletcher, we have a situation," Daniel says, clearing his throat and sitting at the head of the table. "We need to get Heather to settle immediately so your brother can finalize his divorce."

28

Hunter

After a tumultuous dinner at my parents' house, I'm feeling restless again. It seems I don't even get to enjoy a few hours of bliss in my newfound relationship with Abigail.

I take Abigail's hand and lead her out of the house into the back yard while Diana and Archer help clean up. Long ago, my father carved a wooden bench and placed it under the willow tree at the back of the garden. Their property borders the creek, and the running water makes for a pleasant backdrop. I used to love to sit here alone and gather my thoughts, to study the shifting leaves throughout the seasons and observe the changes in my father's garden based on the weather cycles.

"I used to collect acorns from the oaks along the creek," I tell Abigail. "I'd bring them back here, take them apart, and study the differences between the burr oak and the water oak acorn. And my father was always here to listen to my discoveries." I pull Abigail's hand into mine, lacing my fingers between hers and tugging her close against me on the bench. The autumn night is chilly, but I don't want to go back inside. "I used to think my parents' marriage was convenient like mine and Heather's. Dad stayed home with us and mom worked. They each seemed to have separate roles in our family and they seem very content with their division of labor."

Abigail nods.

"I have since realized they share something much deeper," I tell her. "My parents understand each other, help to bring out the things the other person most needs. They fit together, like cytosine and guanine."

"I don't know what those words mean, Hunter."

I sigh. "They just...complement each other. They're partners."

We both look in the window, where my father drops a kiss on my mother's forehead and changes the song on the stereo. They talk softly together while they both work to scour the roasting pan from the chicken. "Heather and I didn't have a partnership, though," I continue. "We had separate lives and...tolerated each other."

Abigail sighs. "I think I can relate to that," she says, telling me a bit about the beginnings of her relationship with Jack. In some ways, our lives were parallel before she came to Oak Creek. It's hard for me to understand her parents wanting her to sacrifice her own ambitions, her own skills, for the family business, but I also see that my father left his career for the sake of Rose Mitchell's ambition.

"But Hunter," she says, "Your father seems like he made that choice willingly. And your siblings have been independent for a long enough time that Daniel could have returned to some sort of career if he felt inclined."

She shivers, and I rise, tugging her to her feet. "Let's go home," I suggest. I rap my knuckles on the kitchen window and wave to my parents. We walk together to my house, with Abigail tucked under my arm.

"Will you stay with me again tonight," she asks, her voice filled with hopefulness even I can identify. I nod and, as we climb the steps to her room, I contemplate the logistics of carving a doorway between our houses on the second floor.

Being in a relationship with Abigail is so much easier than simply desiring Abigail. I feel regret at not telling her about my feelings sooner. She seems to wake up each morning ravenous for sex, and I find that beginning my day with this type of release makes me a much more pleasant instructor at the college. My students seem less tense, even with the mid-term exam approaching.

I explained to Abigail that it's hard for me to see her wearing tight clothing and bending to lift weights without overpowering lust. She alternates between wanting to have sex immediately after work, before we exercise, or else teasing me and forcing me to watch her deadlift in spandex before letting me devour her on the floor. I love letting her dictate the when and where and how of our sex life, and having this control seems to make her feel even better. It's a cycle that just builds until I get to see her come multiple times a day.

I'm so caught up in Abigail that I forget to plan my caloric intake. We eat our dinners together on her couch, our legs entwined as she tells me about her favorite television programs. We play a game where we try to predict the answer to the final question on *Jeopardy* before Alex reveals the clue, and I feel delighted when Abigail correctly guesses the Panama Canal.

Each evening, we lie in her beautiful bed with our laptops. The draft she created of my research proposal is so well-argued, so persuasive. I swell with pride at the idea that this woman is my partner, this brilliant communication strategist. In the few months she's been in town, she has helped reformed my mother's fundraising for the college, prepared me to present my work to an investor, and apparently helped set up a way for my sister to sell alcohol during the Autumn Apple festival this weekend.

"I already cannot imagine life without you, Abigail," I tell her one night after she turns off the light. I had just achieved a personal objective to bring her to orgasm three times in one lovemaking session and I revel in the sight of her limp-limbed bliss. She smiles lazily and runs a hand through my hair. She drifts off to sleep in my arms and I am happily bewildered by how content I feel to be here with her. How lucky I am that fortune brought her to Oak Creek.

29

Abigail

Hunter turns out to be a fantastic boyfriend. As long as I am meticulously clear about what I need and want and expect. Sometimes I feel frustrated that he doesn't take it for granted he should tell me if he's going to play cards with his brother after work…I also have to remember things are moving pretty quickly with him.

I'm not sure if it's a blessing or a curse that we live on opposite sides of a duplex. I've now combed over Hunter's entire half of our building, and between the mattress on the floor in his room and the increasingly smelly weight lifting equipment in the dining room, I'm pretty insistent that we spend most of our time on my half.

I know we've only been together a short time, but I can already see how he gets engrossed in his work. I try not to take it personally or smother him. But I also decide that it's perfectly acceptable for his girlfriend to come visit him in his lair while he's busy being the mad scientist.

Not that he would ever dream of conflating romance with his lab space. His microscope is sacred to him. Regardless, I can't contain my excitement when I finally pin down a date with Asa Wexler, the investor, so I duck into Hunter's lab late one afternoon to share the news in person.

My breath catches when I see him bent over his microscope. He's so focused, moving his samples around delicately, muttering to himself while he takes notes on what he sees. I don't want to startle him, so I slide up behind him and say his name gently.

"Hunter."

He spins slowly on his stool and smiles. I step toward him, standing in between his legs. This is pretty hot. I put my hands on his shoulders and fiddle with his collar. "What brings you in here, Abigail?"

In lieu of answering, I start to hitch up my skirt. "What's happening?" He asks, eyes wide.

"Well," I tell him, slowly unbuttoning his shirt. I like how he looks, all tucked in and put together. I can't wait to make him come apart. "I have news."

"Is the news related to or separate from the sexual things you are doing right now?" He honks my breasts and looks up at me, hopefully.

"We have a date that Mr. Wexler is coming to campus—December 7—and I managed to schedule you a lunch with him. Just the two of you."

"Just us? You won't be there?"

This makes me pause. "You want me there for your big pitch? I don't even know anything about cellular biology…"

Hunter places his hands on my shoulders. "Neither does Wexler. That's the whole point. I need someone else who knows how to talk to people."

I pull his hand up to my face and kiss his palm. "I know this is very important to you, Hunter."

"Exceedingly important."

"If you want me to come with you, I'll be there. We're a team, right?"

He nods. "Thank you, Abigail. I don't know how to thank you enough."

Shirking out of my top and tossing off my bra, I inch closer to his chest. "I can think of a few ways," I tell him, drawing his strong hands back to my skin, sighing as he moves immediately to perform magic on my nipples.

"I never imagined bringing a woman into the lab before," he says, eyes focused on my stiffening peaks. He looks up to see me licking my lips. I'm already practically panting.

"Dr. Crawford," I say. "I'm going to need you to fuck me here."

He yanks me onto his lap, the seams of my skirt straining as my legs spread wide to wrap around his waist on the stool. He nips at my neck as my head drops back. I'm fully exposed for him except for the skirt bunched up at my waist. "I need to put my slides back before we continue," he says, turning in the stool, not moving me from his lap. I can feel his cock bulging hard between us, pulling at his khaki pants.

Hunter keeps one arm around my waist to steady me and gently removes the slide from the microscope. He pulls open a drawer and I feel a rush of cold air. "The samples are cryogenically frozen," he says, licking at my shoulder and throat while he files his samples. "There." He nudges the drawer shut with his knee. "Now you're my only specimen."

I squeak as Hunter lifts me up and places me on the table. "It's so cold," I say, shivering as he lowers me back.

"I can help," Hunter says, snapping on a pair of gloves. I wasn't sure what direction we were headed, but I'm definitely into it as Hunter slides his hands up my legs, tugs down my panties and tosses them across the room. "I've been wanting to study you, Abigail. I want to see everything about you."

I feel something cold and I look down to see Hunter dabbing a slide against my pulsing center. He kisses me as he presses the glass lid onto the slide, and then he wheels over to his microscope and looks into the eyepiece. "I knew it," he breathes. "You're alive for me, Abigail. Vibrant, flowing with life. Beautiful."

When he looks back at me, his eyes are wild, heady with lust. He moves to take off his gloves, but I grab his wrist. "Leave them on," I pant, grinning, and Hunter nods, returning his fingers to the spot I need them most. "Yes, Dr. Crawford," I moan as he slips a sheathed finger inside. "Just like that."

By the time Hunter whips me into white-hot ecstasy on the table, I can't really focus on my surroundings any longer. Eventually, he stands and nudges me to the edge of the table. Standing between my legs, he unzips his pants and pulls out his cock. I see it twitching, weeping with the same excitement I feel. He looks around the room, pausing. "I don't have a condom here," he says, continuing to stroke himself.

"I have an IUD!" There's no way I'm leaving this room without Hunter fucking me.

He nods, considering. "I had extensive medical testing before going into space," he says.

"Jesus Christ, Hunter, please fuck me."

He grins, then, and places a gloved hand on my thigh. "Abigail," he scolds. "In this room, I prefer to be called Dr. Crawford." And then I gasp as he crashes into me. Gone is the gentle lover from my bedroom. This is like wild Hunter on the dining room floor, ramped up to one thousand. He starts to sweat and I can feel his heart race as he pounds into me on the table. He leans over me, fondling my breasts while he hammers his hips. I love every rough thrust.

"Abigail," he pants. "You drive me mad. You're so slick and tight."

My fists claw mindlessly at his chest, seeking purchase in his shirt as I feel another orgasm building. Just as Hunter begins to swell inside me, his rock-hard shaft growing bigger, I topple over the edge, shouting his name, not caring who hears.

"Yes," he growls. "Gaahh!" And then I feel his release pulsing, spurting inside me. It seems endless, the powerful rush of all that he has, emptying into me alongside his whispers of devotion and adoration.

Later, after we've both put ourselves back together and I declined Hunter's offered alcohol wipes for my nether regions, I ask him what he saw on the slide he made during our table session. "Lactobacillus bacteria, mostly," he says. "But it was *your* lactobacillus bacteria, with your unique blend of amino acids and proteins." He kisses my knuckles. "I can't wait to learn about every cell of your being, Abigail."

And, odd as that seems, I recognize this as Hunter Crawford's highest sign of devotion.

30

Hunter

Friday, I whistle absentmindedly as I pass out the midterm exams to my students. Just about everything in my life is going right at the moment.

I've had two blissful weeks with Abigail.

Last night, we walked outside together at midnight to watch the lunar eclipse. The moon, full and low in the sky, turned red as it crossed orbital paths with the Earth. I felt inspired to share with her some of the observations I made from the space station when I wasn't engrossed in my lab work. I held Abigail close and told her what it was like to see the Earth from outside it, how small and insignificant I felt and had to remind myself that I was up there to make an impact.

"You've impacted my life," she told me, and kissed my neck.

Abigail sent along more information about Asa Wexler's impending visit to campus. He's meeting with my mother to discuss a partnership with the computer science department. They're developing some sort of artificial intelligence technology he's interested in, but most of his investments are related to pharmaceuticals and healthcare. I think he could be a great fit to fund my tissue research, and he agreed. He seems eager for our lunch this winter.

I celebrate by setting an exam that's much more rigorous than I would have written otherwise. I already know the students are terrified. But if they want to make a difference in the world, they simply must develop a strong foundation. They cannot be impactful biologists without this level of rigor, and I tell them so.

The students groan, reading the essay question I created for them. "Oh, come now," I tell them. "You all should know by now how cell cycles are dependent on one another. And Khalil, don't look at me like that. I know you know about energy conversion in Eykaryotic cells."

I pull out my phone to set it on airplane mode while they take their exam and then I gaze at photographs of Abigail. My favorite is the picture of her asleep, her dark hair falling off the side of the bed, her plump lips turned up in a smile.

Despite Ed Hastings' attempt to derail our relationship, Abigail and I are on a strong trajectory toward happiness. Even Diana seems to approve.

Eventually, my timer goes off and the students groan. They bring their papers to the front as I assure them everything will be fine. One bad exam in a biology class isn't going to damage their future, statistically speaking. "Besides," I tell them. "I had a 4.0 and I still managed to get fired from the Space Agency."

This doesn't quite elicit the laugh I had been going for. Abigail says I still need to work on my deliberate jokes.

I spend the next hour grading exams, fighting off the nagging sense that I'm supposed to be doing something else, but then Moorely raps on the doorway and asks me to have a drink with him. Considering my excitement at my upcoming meeting with Wexler, I actually do feel like having a beer with Moorely. He's familiar with these sorts of meetings, and I feel more confident after running some of my ideas past him at the Nobler Experiment.

A few hours later, it occurs to me that I haven't touched base with Abigail. When I pull out my phone to call her, I see that it's still on airplane mode. I hadn't wanted it to ring or vibrate during my students' exam.

"Oh no. Oh. No, oh no oh no." I was supposed to spend the afternoon helping with Autumn Apple. I look around the bar, which is nearly empty save for us. And no wonder—half the town is out with my family, working to set up the festival booths. How could I have forgotten this commitment?

Even Moorely picks up on my distress when I turn the phone back on and see the stream of missed calls and messages. "What did you forget to do, mate?"

I exhale slowly through my nose. "I was supposed to help Abigail set up for the festival," I tell him. She's been expecting me for at least four hours, and I've been grading papers and drinking with Moorely. I feel a wave of shame at how quickly I slipped back into old habits, at how much I dislike this aspect of my personality. "What am I going to do, Moorely?"

This is going to take some work to atone for.

31

Abigail

Friday morning dawns bright and crisp. The perfect weather to set up the Autumn Apple festival. The small town has already been transformed. Main Street is lined with hay bales and gourd displays. Each small business, from the Houseplant Haven to the animal clinic to even the co-op, has a wooden booth set up on the sidewalk.

The festival includes apple bobbing, apple artwork, apple-themed crafts for sale. The tai chi group has developed a routine in honor of the apple harvest. Some of the elderly women in town embroidered apple blossoms on beautiful silk pillowcases. I make a mental note to buy a set, imagining how they'll feel against my cheek while I'm rolling around in my bed with Hunter.

Despite our nose dive into the insatiable phase of our relationship, I feel comfortable in my life with him. Which is not to say I feel like I'm settling.

I spoke with my parents earlier in the week. They admitted that things have been fine in the business—they hired someone else to work in the office, and she's doing a fine job. They still seem to think I'm going to come home and patch things up with Jack, who is evidently now working nights as a security guard at the bank.

I asked them not to call me again for awhile. I need some time to figure out how to mend a relationship with a family who simply will not see that I've made a positive change in my life. That seems to be the beauty of Oak Creek. People are supported in their desires to change...unless it involves archaic alcohol laws.

Looking around the festival, at all the volunteers looking to me for direction and helping to fold the brochures and festival programs that I created, I feel pride in what I've accomplished and sadness that my own family won't know or see that I can do big things.

Our staging ground for setup is at Sara's law office, which is in the same building as Archer Crawford's CPA office. The parking lot is crawling with Crawfords hauling crates of apples, boxes of wrist bands. I hear Indigo explaining sperm donation to a fascinated Archer. "It's gonna come in a giant tank," Indigo says. "They ship it on dry ice. Sara's going to squirt it in me at our house."

"Now how does that work," he says, counting out a stack of aprons for the different shifts of Autumn Apple staffers. "Is it really a turkey baster situation?"

Indigo laughs. "More like a syringe, silly." I clear my throat. "Abigail! Yay! Now we can really get going." Indigo rushes over to me with marching orders. Soon all thoughts of my family drama slip away and I work up a sweat as we all set up the booths.

After lunch I start checking my watch, counting down the minutes until Hunter gets here to help. I'm eager for his assistance, but mostly I just miss him. It feels strange since we share a roof and have been spending all our time together.

But he's so supportive and, when he remembers to say his thoughts out loud, he says the most wonderful, earnest things about what he enjoys about my brain, my body, and the way I massage his balls.

I smile, flushing, as I remember his intense stare this morning, when he said, "Abigail, I never knew how good it would feel for someone to pinch my epididymus."

My smile gives way to growing anxiety when Hunter is not here by 4. I know his students finished their midterm exam an hour before, and he was meant to help hoist the heavy kegs of hard cider from the delivery truck.

"Where's my damn brother," Diana hollers, grunting under the weight of one of the kegs.

"He's not answering his phone," I admit, adding embarrassment to my list of emotions simmering to the surface the longer he goes without contacting us. The sting of spoiled expectations blends with my concern for where he could be. I hate this feeling of not knowing, of wondering whether I should worry or be irritated that he just forgot.

"Fuck it," Diana says. She strips off her sweater and powers through the unloading on her own. Her muscles flex as she rage-lifts enough alcohol for an entire town for tomorrow's festival. I try to help her, but even after months working out with Hunter, I'm not strong enough to do more than topple a keg to its side. "Don't roll it, Abigail. It'll explode."

I sink onto a hay bale feeling dejected while Diana finishes. "Listen," she says, guzzling the water bottle I hand her. It's after dark by now and my teeth chatter, but Diana stands in the glow of the twinkle lights, sweating. "My brother always does this shit. He gets focused on his microscope and the rest of the world melts away. I don't think it's on purpose, but I also don't think he's going to change." She tosses the empty bottle in the recycling bin by the front of the booth and pats me on the shoulder. "I'm going home to shower. Get some rest. We're going to sling a lot of apples tomorrow, girl."

After Diana leaves, I'm alone at the cider booth. The rest of the crew mills around nearby, and every now and then Sara gestures thumbs up, thumbs down, questioning whether I'm ok over here. I flash her a thumb sideways and sit down to consult my checklist. I think we got everything ready. I should feel proud of the work I did, of the way this small town embraced me into the fold and we all collaborated to make something that looks like a storybook. Everything is sparkling with twinkle lights. The scents of cinnamon and cloves permeate the air from the pie booths and slow cookers full of fresh apple cider, set to simmer overnight for the morning crowd.

Tomorrow is going to be amazing. *Despite Hunter Crawford,* I think, angrily.

No longer able to process my disappointment in public, I start toward home, letting the tears well up and looking forward to locking myself inside to sob.

Diana is right—I knew this about him. And yet, here I am, deeply upset and rattled by something my new boyfriend did. Or didn't do. I can't even concentrate at this point.

I should never have gotten so intimate with Hunter so quickly. I should have worked harder to take things slowly, kept it light so I wasn't this gutted when he stood me up. Then I remind myself that he stood up the whole town and his family. Diana said he does this all the time. Maybe accepting Hunter as a flake is part of accepting him.

Just as I'm wrestling with all these thoughts, I see Hunter and his friend Moorely approaching. And they're each carrying a chicken.

Moorely seems out of breath and flustered, holding his chicken upside-down by its feet as it flaps and squawks. "Abigail," he huffs. "Here." He thrusts the bird into my arms and storms off toward Archer, shouting, "Oy! Other-Crawford! Tell me you've got something over in that dunk tank to scrub chicken shit off my trainers."

I look down at the bird in my arms, who has calmed down now that I'm holding her more like a baby, cradled in one arm. She looks up at me as if she's confused, too.

When I meet Hunter's eyes, I can't help myself. I start crying, whether from relief or anger or confusion, I can't tell. "I'm really angry at you, Hunter!" I sniff, unable to wipe away my tears while I'm holding the bird.

"Abigail, I owe you an apology," he says, petting the bird tucked under his arm. Both chickens are speckled, with soft black and white feathers and a bright red comb. Hunter nods his chin in the direction of my hen. "I brought these as a symbol of my commitment to do better."

"I don't understand, Hunter. Where did you get chickens?"

"Well, I took them from my father," he says, shifting his weight and passing the chicken to the other side. "Look, can we walk home and I promise to explain?"

Only because I am so taken aback by the presence of a pair of chickens do I let him convince me to walk with him along the creek.

When we reach a muddy patch on the bank he stoops and puts his bird down, gesturing that I should do so, too. The girls begin pecking around in the mud, extracting plump worms and happily slurping them down in the moonlight. "I tend to do things like this," Hunter says. "I get absorbed in my work and then I let people down."

"So I see." I nudge a pebble with my toe until one of the hens comes and pecks at it, evidently thinking it's a beetle. "I don't want to be someone's second priority, Hunter. I mean, you didn't even call."

"Tonight I had actually finished my work when Moorely showed up for a drink, and because I'm not in the practice of acting like part of a team, I went with him." I open my mouth to interject something angry, but he continues. "But I want to do better, Abigail. That's the difference you've made in my life. You make me want to improve this aspect of myself. I am committing to do better. This is my vow."

"Hunter, I'm sorry, but I just don't see what stealing your father's chickens has to do with a commitment to anything." I feel myself growing more angry the more he talks about chatting with his British buddy while Diana single-handedly unloaded a truck of heavy kegs.

"I'm getting there." He sighs. "This is new to me—expressing my feelings and...caring whether another person understands my motivations." I see him swallow, illuminated by the moon. "I thought having a pet could help me. If there's always a living being at home who requires my care, I can't let my own work overpower my thoughts. And I thought of a chicken because, well, you have to be there every day to collect the eggs or they get broody."

Hunter steps closer to me. "Broody?"

He nods. "These are my chickens, Abigail. I don't want you to think I'll just get absent-minded and leave you with additional work. This is my commitment to begin living a life that considers others." He raises his eyebrows as he extends his arms, asking silent permission to touch me. I step into his embrace and he pulls me tight, whispering into my ear that he wants to gather eggs for me every morning, and be present to make sure the birds have water each night before bed.

"My dad told me it was ok to take them," he murmurs. "He has plenty."

32

Hunter

I hadn't planned my chicken gesture very carefully. I don't have a coop or anything to keep the girls safe from raccoons, and so I decide to put them in my house since I don't really have anything downstairs.

Abigail suggests I move my computer equipment upstairs so the birds don't shit on my keyboard. I'm reminded again how wonderful it is to have someone at my side who can think of these details. I need to work as hard as it takes to keep her.

I've managed to earn her forgiveness this time, and I don't intend to have to try again. With the chickens clucking happily around a bowl of corn, Abigail and I head to bed, where she seems very pleased at my offer of a shoulder massage.

As a gesture of my commitment, I attend the Autumn Apple festival with her bright and early the next morning. I do not voice my dislike of crowds or other humans and consciously work to overcome those feelings. I try to focus on Abigail and how much she is enjoying her Autumn Apple debut.

I stay by her side the entire day as she cheerily sells apples to all the townspeople, who introduce themselves to her as they chug hard cider in front of the library. The Acorns start on the cider early, and by the time they begin their special Tai Chi demonstration, they're all teetering a bit. Abigail raises her eyebrows at me when some of the Acorns stop by the apple cider booth to thank me for the Kivin method.

"It was a good article worth sharing," I tell her, nodding to Mary Pat when she ducks out of the co-op for more "donations" from Abigail's cider keg.

Soon, half the town is gathered around Abigail, staring at us. I keep my arm securely around her, massaging her arm while she flushes, and assure them all that the *Gazette* article got almost everything wrong.

"But you really did buy the jumbo pack of condoms?" Enid, the constable, stares wide-eyed in fascination at the thought that someone could have enough sex to warrant purchasing the large box from Oak Creek Drug.

Mary Pat slings an arm around Enid's shoulders and points at me with her cider cup. "Of course he needed the jumbo pack. Dr. Crawford is who got Lamar to go downtown." She waggles her eyebrows drunkenly, and I begin to seriously consider whether I should start a lecture series at the college about the anatomy of the vulva.

My mother comes floating by the cider booth a few hours later, escorting the foreign alumni she's got staying in my brother's old bedroom. "Hiiiii!" She says, waving at us merrily. "Bruno, Angelica, this is my oldest son, Hunter, and my senior communications strategist, Abigail. We have her to thank for almost everything smart I say." Ma's guests laugh and Abigail hands them cider after verifying they're over 21.

Abigail accepts approximately 15 offers to have dinner or coffee with various locals, turns away scores of undergraduate students, including half of mine, and beams with delight as Archer hauls away a third crate of cash to the safe he's got in his office for all the festival funds.

"What are we earning money for anyway? I never asked..."

I shrug. "I always just thought it paid for the fireworks," I tell her.

As darkness falls, my father comes over to the cider booth holding a plaid blanket. He drapes it over Abigail's shoulders and tells her the entire town thinks she's the best thing to come to Oak Creek since sliced gluten-free bread arrived at the co-op.

"Hey, Dad," I ask as he prepares to take over for Abigail so she and I can wander around the festival. "Can you help me build a coop for the chickens tomorrow?"

"Son," he says, grinning. "There's nothing I'd enjoy more." Abigail and I start to walk off, holding hands—something I've never particularly desired before but suddenly don't want to stop. Dad hollers to stop us, saying, "Oh, Hunter, Sara said she wanted to talk with you."

Abigail and I roam the Autumn Apple festival, planning to see Sara before the fireworks. Abigail stops for a funnel cake, and I bite back the urge to explain how awful such foods are for her metabolism and cardiovascular health. Sometimes a treat just tastes good, I decide, and take a nibble of the fatty, sugary dough. Abigail pulls me down for a kiss, licking powdered sugar from the corner of my mouth and sending me into a state of arousal that has me looking for the nearest dark alley where we can retreat.

Resisting the carnal urge and wanting to hear Sara's news, I stop by the apple bobbing stand near the Inn. I promise Abigail to bob with her in the bin filled with other people's saliva, just as soon as I talk with Sara. Abigail rolls her eyes and joins an intoxicated Mary Pat at the galvanized tub of bacteria water, leaving me to chat with my lawyer.

"Hunter!" Sara grins. She holds up her phone. "We got them." Sara tells me that Heather's legal team has reached an agreement—a payout that seems extremely reasonable. No further claims on my future patents. No ongoing alimony. A lump sum and I can move on with my life.

I clear my throat and try to temper the swell of emotion I feel at finally being able to finalize my divorce. "Sara," I say. "I just...thank you."

"Ah, come here, you dumb genius," Sara says, rising to her feet. She pulls me in to a bear hug, pounding me on the back. I glance over to Abigail, and gesture for her to join the hug until the three of us are spinning around the fading glow of the Autumn Apple festival.

"Good news?" she asks.

"Definitely satisfactory," I say, planting a kiss on her forehead and inhaling the sunshine and cinnamon scents lingering around her.

"Ladies and gentlemen," Ed Hastings' voice comes over the megaphone and the tittering crowd slowly quiets. "It is now time for the annual Autumn Apple Harvest Fireworks. Please enjoy this year's display, and remember. Open containers of alcohol are absolutely prohibited in Oak Creek. Our constable may be incapacitated at the moment, but our laws are still in force!"

I guide Abigail over to a nearby hay bale and pull her against me to watch the display. I've always enjoyed fireworks. Chemistry wasn't my preferred science, but I have always appreciated the beautiful reactions when the barium chloride and strontium carbonate light up green and red. "You know," I whisper to Abigail in between launches, "I was in the Space Station over the 4th of July. A lot of the astronauts watched the fireworks on the Internet, but I didn't want to leave the lab. There's not a great sense of time passing up there anyway."

"That sounds sad, Hunter," she says.

"Well," I tell her, slipping her another kiss as one of the starburst fireworks sizzles, "I was up in the galley very late, and we happened to be orbiting over the US at the time. It was a clear night, so when I stood at the window, I really thought I saw the faint glow of fireworks over the southwest, where there's no other light pollution. It was a really nice moment of connection. Made me think of being home, just like this."

Only then, I didn't know that home could feel this way. As it turns out, that would have been right when my wife was leaving me, turning my life upside down. Really, though, she was just adjusting my trajectory toward home. I had no way of knowing then that I could have a woman by my side who wanted to be there. Who I wanted desperately to stay in my orbit.

As the finale begins, I tug Abigail to her feet, gesturing my head toward home. I feel a desperate urge to make love to her. I can't even speak as I pull her in the front door and carry her up the stairs. I try to let my kisses express the words I cannot summon, gently pressing my lips against hers, softly caressing her tongue with my own.

"Oh, Hunter," she sighs, and I love hearing my name on her lips. I undress her quickly and kick off my clothes. Abigail lies on her back and crawls up the bed, beckoning me to lie on top of her. As I settle in between her legs, I hear the final crack of the fireworks, followed by a crack of thunder. I briefly look up from my lady to see the flash of lightning out the window, but I like how the gentle rain forms background music for the symphony I want to create in here with Abigail.

She rocks her hips beneath me, urging me to enter her, and I exhale as I slide home. Abigail is always so wet and ready for me, so eager to pull me inside deeper, deeper, and deeper again. "More," she whispers into my ear, and the feel of her breath against my skin sends shivers through me. Abigail wraps her arms around me, holding me tight against her naked chest.

This moment is so intense. I feel absolutely vulnerable and yet totally powerful all at once. In another flash of lightning I see Abigail's face melting in delight, feeling pleasure that I am bringing to her, that she says is due to me being with her. "Abigail, I am yours," I groan, feeling her body contract against me as she comes, moaning my name.

The pulsing, tight warmth of her body sends me soaring into my own ecstasy, and

I come, gushing inside her, wanting to stay connected to her always. Afterward, I don't rush out of bed to clean up. I don't even want to do that. I roll gently to Abigail's side and pull her against my body, raining kisses on her as she catches her breath.

33

Abigail

"I'll give you my entire next paycheck if I don't have to come clean up wet hay," I moan into my phone when Indigo calls in the morning. I was too busy making love all night to worry about what cleanup would be like in the morning.

"All part of the planning committeee," she chides. "Besides, I'll take you to the salt cave after."

One of the shops along Main Street, Oak Clarity Crystals, has a salt cave in the back. It's really just a room in her store building, but Melody's lined the walls and ceiling with Himalayan pink salt, creating a "healing cave." Indigo has been trying to get me to go sit in there with her, to boost my immune system and revitalize my skin.

Hunter says he has to deal with some paperwork and meet his father this morning anyway, so I begrudgingly put on my rattiest clothes to go help take down the Autumn Apple festival. I smile, tying my hair up in a bun, thinking about how he lay on top of me as we listened to the rain, sliding inside me so gently, moving along with the surges of the cloud bursts.

I suspect I won't see him for awhile today, since he didn't check on his tissue samples at all yesterday. He left in a hurry, and I realize I never got a chance to ask him the details of what happened with Sara and his legal situation.

As it turns out, a large number of Oak Creekers have shown up to gather the hay bales and decorative gourds for the animal rescue. Diana has a composting operation set up for anything damaged by the storm to feed to the rescued rabbits or line the cat cages. The Acorns, spry and miraculously not hungover, have already taken down the wooden booths and hauled them back to the storage shed at the edge of town. It's barely ten AM and already, it looks like the festival never happened.

Mary Pat got emergency approval from the co-op board to pass out sprouted wheat muffins and fresh carrot juice to all the volunteers, and by lunchtime, I find myself tilted back in a zero-gravity chair beside Indigo, basking in the pink glow of the salt cave.

"How long do we stay in here," I ask her, slurping the rest of my juice. I'm pretty sure Mary Pat added tequila to mine, because I feel woozy, but I roll with it, letting my body relax after an exhausting few days.

Indigo shrugs and stretches her hands above her head. "I think like a half hour? I want to come every day to get my body ready for pregnancy," she says, grinning. "Now that the festival's over we don't have anything big to plan until Operation Kringle in December." She pauses. "I guess that's only a month. But anyway! I'm going to make time to sit in this cave, dang it."

"Should I ask about Operation Kringle?"

"Probably not."

Relaxed and salted, I make my way home by way of the co-op, where I pick up grilled chicken strips and fresh veggies to make Hunter a salad. I think about how nice it felt to go with him at dawn and visit the chickens, find where they'd laid their eggs on his computer chair. The birds really are a nice gesture, I decide.

And, even though they're supposed to be his responsibility to take care of, I really want to visit them. They're interesting and friendly. He hasn't called at all today, so I assume he's pretty involved in whatever he's working on with his dad.

I stop in my half of the duplex to put away the groceries and grab some apples that have gone past their prime. I figure the chickens won't mind, and I walk through the yard to tug open Hunter's back door.

I freeze in my tracks when I see a woman standing at his counter, writing something. She looks up at me, one sculpted eyebrow raised derisively. "And just who are you?" she asks, coldly.

I'm so stunned I almost answer her, and then I realize there's no one who should be standing in Hunter's house. "I should be asking you that question," I retort.

One of the chickens squawks and flaps her wings, and I stoop to give her one of the apples. "Here you go, girl," I say, patting the industrious chicken while the stranger stands, legs spread, stilettoed toe tapping the mat near a pile of chicken shit.

"I see Hunter hasn't picked up any more housekeeping skills since I left," she says, running her finger along a small pile of feathers on the counter. "You can see how much he needs me. It's good that I'm back." The birds flap and she backs up. "We'll find someplace befitting a scientist of his calibre." She smiles an icy smile, and I realize this is Hunter's ex-wife.

"Wait," I say, dropping the rest of the apples to the chickens. "You're supposed to be signing divorce papers."

She tilts her head to the side, pouting mockingly. "Is that what they told you? Aw, sorry." She walks closer to me. She's at least six inches taller than me, so she's literally looking down her nose at me as she says, "Don't think I don't know about Hunter's little *diversion* here in Oak Creek. But I can assure you, we are very much still married." She flashes her left hand in my face and I see a gaudy, giant diamond ring on her manicured finger.

None of this makes sense. "I think I'd better call Hunter," I say, reaching for my phone.

Heather snorts. "Go ahead. Call my husband back to this *dump* so we can get out of here faster. We're both eager to get reacquainted after our little misunderstanding."

She stalks back to the counter where she begins gathering the papers she'd been writing on when I arrived. "Oh, and by the way," she says. "I hear tell I have you to thank for teaching Hunter some new tricks." She winks and I want to simultaneously claw her eyes out and vomit on the floor with the chicken shit. "Our reunion is shaping up to be sensational."

I glance behind Heather toward the living room area and see a few black suitcases packed by the door. My head is pounding and my thoughts are racing. Could Hunter have truly gotten back together with his wife in the few hours since we were last together? He seemed so open last night, so committed to me. But then I remember the article Ed Hastings wrote, where he implied Hunter would do anything to avoid a huge divorce payout. *Surely that didn't include taking back the woman who left him while he was on a mission in outer space?*

I know Heather had been really trying to rake him over the coals in the divorce, and that he wasn't objecting to paying her—I can see now she's the kind of woman who requires a lot of money for her upkeep—but I heard she was also trying to make sure she got money from his future research patents. The thought of her trying to profit from his research, trying to steal his brilliant passion…it pisses me off.

"Look, Heather—"

"No, you look." She whips her head around. "I put up with his bullshit for years. I cleaned for him. Arranged his calendar. I did everything, everything so that he could pursue his research. So he could stretch that brilliant mind of his into the universe and back. And I'll be damned if I put in all that work just so some skank in ripped leggings can reap the reward. So why don't you let yourself out the way you came in and leave me here with my husband to work out the details of our reconciliation."

I don't say a word, slamming the back door behind me as I rush into my apartment and collapse in angry sobs.

34

Hunter

I feel weightless as I walk to my parents' house from Sara's office. Signing those papers feels like lifting the last bit of gravity dragging my past along with me.

I never said I was a good husband. Hell, I was probably a lousy human being to Heather, and I don't mind giving her a payout. My townhouse here is fully paid for and I have Abigail's rent coming in each month on top of my teaching salary. I'll be just fine.

Thanks to Sara, my future intellectual property is mine alone. Heather has no further ties to me. None.

The world seems bright and filled with possibilities as my father and I get to work building a small coop for the chickens. I meant what I said to Abigail, that I want to make sure I have multiple reminders not to let myself get buried in my work again. I don't want to go back to being that person, who selfishly pursues my own obsessions about science at the expense of my relationships with other people. I even have been enjoying spending time with Moorely, now that I understand his humor a bit more.

"Son, I want you to know I think Abigail is a really good match for you." Dad talks without making eye contact as he makes measurements and marks the wood with a pencil. "Your mom and I are so glad to see you happy."

"You can tell that I'm happy?" I look around as if I have a mark on my clothes somehow.

Dad chuckles and looks up. "I can, Hunter. And not just because you're smiling all the time now. You're also grumbling less and I haven't even seen you pacing in months."

"Hm." I do those things, it's true—grumble to myself and pace. I don't know that I considered those were markers of unhappiness. Restlessness. "You'd make a good researcher, Dad."

He flips down his safety glasses and lines a plank up by the circular saw. "Been there, Hunter. Tried that." He looks at me for a minute, considering. "Then you came along, and your mother and I were caught off guard. It seemed a more important and worthwhile challenge to stay home and figure out how to help you become...well, just become."

My parents don't talk a lot about my dad's decision to stay home with us 32 years ago. He often says he likes redirecting his analytical energy into making a home for 4 kids and that studying our mother is a career unto itself.

I'm not sure what to make of this revelation that my arrival was the catalyst for his life changing, but then I remember all the catalysts that brought me and Abigail to where we are right now. Dad starts drilling planks together and I fall in step beside him. I said I didn't want anything fancy or ornate, but by the time Dad calls Archer to borrow his truck for the finished coop, we've made the chickens luxurious nesting boxes inside, with easy-access flaps at the bottom for egg retrieval. Dad decides it's prudent to add a light fixture, too, in case of extreme cold. I don't bother to tell him the chickens are currently in my dining room. I suppose it's not good practice to default to having the chickens inside the house.

Archer arrives and admires the coop, smacking me on the back and then hugging Dad. The three of us put the coop in Archer's truck bed and squeeze into the cab. When we pull up to my house, I see a familiar Lexus parked out front, and my chest tightens. "Wait here," I say to my dad and Archer, approaching the front door with trepidation.

If my ex-wife is in my house, I want to get her out of there as quickly as possible. Why the hell would she be in town? We signed the papers electronically via our respective lawyers. Heather shouldn't be anywhere near Oak Creek. I don't even want Abigail to see her on the property, let alone risk her coming across Heather in the back yard or something.

I curse myself for how quickly I returned to the small-town habit of leaving my doors unlocked. While it's convenient leaving the house with no keys, clearly the practice leaves much to be desired in terms of security.

I open the door slowly, and my fears are realized. "Heather," I say, frowning at both her and the bags she seems to have brought inside. "What is this?"

She snorts. "That's the greeting I get? What's it been—a year, Hunter?"

"Well," I say, "we were supposed to see one another in Kazakhstan a few months ago. You decided not to come, as I recall. You were emptying out our condo."

Neither of us speaks for awhile, and I remember how long stretches of silence make her uncomfortable. "What's in the bags, Heather?"

"Oh, those?" She gestures over toward the pile of suitcases. "It's all things I have no use for. Things I took from the condo."

"Ok, well why are they here?"

"Well, don't you want them back? All your special toothpastes and protein powders? I have no further use for them."

"And yet they belong to you, according to the legal documents we both just signed. So I'll ask you again, Heather. What are you doing here? I don't want six-month-old toothpaste."

"Maybe I wanted to give you one more shot to see what you're missing," she says, walking closer. While I never found Heather a turn-off, certainly, I also wouldn't say she ever particularly aroused me, either.

Nothing about our relationship was related to lust, let alone love. Standing near her now, I realize that more than ever before.

"Heather," I say, holding out my hands to ensure she maintains a distance between us. "I've apologized for my part in the destruction of our marriage. I treated you badly, and I am sorry for that. Honestly, I can say that your leaving me was one of the best things that ever happened to me." Her face crumples into rage and I know I've made a mistake. "That came out wrong."

"Fuck you, Hunter." Her voice is cold, calculating. "You think you can just pay me off and I'll fade into the background?"

I roll my eyes. "Yes, actually. And I've got a stack of paperwork indicating you agreed." One of the chickens wanders into the room then and begins to peck at my sneaker. I stoop to pick her up, planting a kiss on her feathered head without thinking. "Look, now you can start fresh..."

Heather stares at me and the chicken, and for the first time, I think I can guess what she is thinking. Heather is upset that I never showed her affection, like I just did so casually with the chicken. She surprises me when she starts to cry quietly, tears rolling down her cheeks.

"I just don't get it," she says. "I came here to sign these papers and move on with my life. I was so sure you were incapable of loving *anyone*. While you were up in that lab, never calling, never contacting me for weeks on end, I assumed that you just don't need human companionship. You were never going to need to be married to me. And so I left."

Heather wipes at her cheek with her hand, sniffing. "But then I came to town to sign the papers. I was on my way to Philadelphia anyway and figured I'd just sign in person, maybe shake your hand and part as friends. But of course everyone in town is talking all about that damn festival last night. Imagine my surprise to hear them whispering, laughing about Hunter Crawford lovesick, infatuated with his new girlfriend."

"Heather—"

"No, you let me finish!" Her voice is raw, barely contained emotion shaking out in her words. "How the hell do you think that makes me feel? Oh, wait. You have no idea, right? You don't understand human emotion. Well, Hunter, it feels like garbage to realize you're not actually a robot. You just didn't give a shit about *me.*"

I am unsure what to do, so I just continue petting the chicken, who pecks at my shirt hopefully while we both wait for Heather to continue. "I loved you once, Hunter. Hunter Crawford, the most brilliant student to grace the halls of MIT in a generation! Paying attention to me in the library, responding to me when I suggested we should go see the Boston Philharmonic. I was *somebody* when I was with you, Hunter, until the person I was without you seemed to fade away. And then at least I convinced myself you needed me. That you'd be living with animals and chicken shit on the floor without me. And you *are* living that way and it doesn't even fucking bother you!"

"Heather, I'm sorry." I sigh and put down the chicken, holding my palms up in submission. "I should never have taken you for granted."

She sniffs, drawing in a jagged breath and wiping away one last line of tears. Her nostrils flare and she shakes her head. I watch her transform back into the cool, distant woman I'm accustomed to. "Well, I appreciate your apology. Please don't contact me. I can show myself out." She climbs over the luggage and the pair of chickens who have now roosted on the pile of bags. I see her taking in my surroundings. I know it looks sparse and pathetic, covered in feathers and animal droppings. But I don't care. The important stuff lies on the other side of the wall anyway.

Heather turns to look at me as she opens the door. She says, "Oh I do hope Abigail isn't too upset after our conversation earlier. The mouth on that girl!"

Before I can accost her and find out precisely what she said to my Abigail, she slams the door in my face and is clicking down the sidewalk. I trip over the stuff in the doorway in my haste to chase after her, and she's in her car driving away before I can get on my feet and out the front door.

Heather talked to Abigail, I think. *Heather must have lied to Abigail. Something is wrong here.*

I walk straight to Abigail's door and knock, but there's no answer. I pull out my phone to call her, frantically, but my call goes directly to voicemail. Her car is gone. The curtains are all drawn and I can't see inside.

"Dad," I shout, jogging around back where he and my brother have just finished setting up the coop.

"Hey, son. Was that Heather I saw leaving?"

"Dad, you have to help me find Abigail."

35

Hunter

Abigail is missing, having encountered Heather, and we have no way of knowing what my ex-wife might have said to her. I predict the conversation centered around my past transgressions and poor behaviors as a spouse, and potentially the suggestion that I intended to rekindle my relationship with Heather rather than surrender my money.

I find my approach to this problem mirrors my work: I rush upstairs to my computer, still set up on the floor to avoid getting shit on by the chickens downstairs, and type out the variables, potential motives, possible solutions to various scenarios. I forget that my father and brother are here with me until I hear Archer talking loudly on his cell phone. I take note that I'm muttering and pacing—the very behaviors my father notices when I'm unhappy. My thoughts are spiraling, too.

"Ma hasn't heard from Abigail," Archer shouts to the house at large. "But they have a meeting on Monday and Rose believes Abigail would not leave her hanging when she's about to meet the prime minister of Sri Lanka. They're setting up an exchange program."

"Your mother is meeting with Sri Lanka? Shit," my father curses and I hear him stomping around. "That means we are hosting. I have to get home, son. Hunter!" He yells upstairs.

"What, Dad? Come on!"

"Hunter, I'm sorry. If I have foreign dignitaries staying at the house I need to get ready. I'm sure you and your brother are more than capable of locating Abigail and correcting any misunderstanding. I have more chickens if you need another peace offering."

And with that, my father takes off out the front door. "Archer," I stare at my brother, desperate. "I can't even map out an algorithm for this."

"Ok, Hunter. Let's think about this. Who do you know that has searching skills?"

"Searching skills?"

Archer shoves me away from the computer, toward the stairs. "Yeah, like surveillance skills or some ninja shit. Don't you know astronauts?"

I ask Archer to summon Moorely and then I check the date on my watch. November 5. I do some mental calculations and realize Digger must be back home by now. His specialty is cyber security, so I'm certain the program has not canceled his research. I sigh deeply, and pull up his number on an old directory file, hoping he wouldn't have changed his number due to notoriety or privacy or otherwise.

I dial the number nervously, and am greeted with, "Holy shit, Crawdad! Never thought I'd hear from your ass again!"

"How did you know it was me?"

"Who do you think you're calling, dude? What's up?"

Within a few hours, we determine that Abigail has left town, and likely several hours earlier. Her car was spotted at the gas station and Mary Pat told Enid who told the Acorns that Abigail had a lot of clothing in the back seat. Abigail arrived in Oak Creek after a falling out, so I hypothesize she has headed back, convinced that I am leaving her for my ex-wife. The difference this time is that I intend to find her and correct this misunderstanding.

Moorely has identified Abigail's Ohio address and Digger has arranged to come get me in his helicopter. My brother points out the absurd cost of such a flight, but Digger insists he can work the adventure into one of his firewall checks and conduct some business in Ohio while I meet with the Bakers.

Archer takes one look at me, still in my coop-building clothes, and insists that I go shower and change if I'm hoping to win over my partner's parents. I acknowledge the merits of this idea, and when I leave the shower, I see that my brother has procured flowers, chocolates, and a small box of eggs from the other chickens in our father's flock. "I want you to be prepared to kiss a lot of ass, Hunter." He pulls me in for a one-armed hug and then drives me over to the high school, where Digger is landing the helicopter on the lacrosse field.

"Crawdad! Come here, asshole!" Digger jumps out of the plane and ducks under the force of the still-slowing blades, running over to pull me into an awkward hug. Hugging is still something foreign to me, except when it comes to Abigail, but I do understand that others wish to embrace one another as I enjoy doing with her. So I allow Austin Digby to pull me into his sweaty body for a moment.

"Archer, Moorely, this is my former colleague, Digger," I say when he releases me. "Digger, let's go." Digger shakes his head and cracks his gum, saluting my brother and friend as he lifts us off the ground.

It takes less than an hour to fly to Ohio, where Digger has evidently arranged to land on an air strip and called for a government car to retrieve us. He says he's off to investigate cyber security on the water treatment center nearby, but offers to drop me at the Baker household. During the entire flight and car ride, I endure him updating me on everything he's been excited about since returning to earth. Food, television, and sex, evidently. I do feel compelled to suggest the Kivin method to him, which seems to astonish and delight him when he looks it up on his phone. "You can make a woman come in 3 minutes this way? You're going to have to debrief me on this later, dude." The car pulls up to a small ranch house. "Thanks for the diversion this afternoon, Crawdad. Good luck!"

I climb out into the fading light of late afternoon and my friend rolls away, with instructions to meet him back at the high school in three hours. Not much time to calculate whether this town offers ride shares, but I can't worry about that right now. I steel myself to interact with angry parents and ring the bell.

A short woman who resembles Abigail answers the door. Her dark, graying hair is in a ponytail, and I can see how Abigail's face might fill out over the years, how she might develop graceful lines. How she might come to look wise. "May I help you?"

"Yes, hello. My name is Dr. Hunter Crawford. I've come to apologize to Abigail."

"Who's at the door, Mae?"

"Some man looking for Abigail."

A tall, thickly muscled man crosses his arms and frowns at me. "Better get in line, son."

"Is Abigail not here?"

Mae and the man who must be Abigail's father exchange a glance. "We haven't seen our daughter in months."

I run a hand across my chin. She didn't flee to her home after her encounter with Heather. This changes everything. "Sir, ma'am, may I come inside?"

I am reluctantly offered iced tea and a seat in the living room while a football game blares in the background. A trio of men resembling Mr. Baker are crammed onto the couch, shouting at the television, where I see the Cleveland team is playing against the Philadelphia team. I'm reminded again how little enthusiasm I feel for these sorts of events, which would have been similar loud productions in my house growing up. Only it would have been my mother on the couch yelling at the officials and my father making chicken salad.

Mr. Baker plunks into his armchair and points at me. "So I'm thinking my daughter was maybe shacked up with you this whole time, God knows where, and you pissed her off and she ran off again?" Mr. Baker doesn't seem the type to mince words, which interestingly sets me more at ease.

"Well, as you say, I did inadvertently anger her and I'm not sure where she went."

"Can you tell us where our daughter has been?" Mae Baker sits beside her husband on the arm chair, wringing her hands. "We've been worried sick."

"I. Well…"

"She left a good job and a good man, with no warning," Mr. Baker interjects. "Jack's been nuts with worry."

"Jack? The man who harmed Abigail?" The mention of his name has me gritting my teeth. Anger blooms inside my chest at the realization Abigail's family is defending the man who caused Abigail to flee in fear.

"What are you talking about, son? Jack loves Abigail."

I make eye contact with Mae and try to delicately phrase my feelings about this perception of events. "He nearly ripped her ear off in a rage and had been isolating her from you for months," I say, steel in my voice, ice in my veins.

Abigail's brothers all turn their head from the television. "Say what, now? Jack laid hands on Abby?"

I briefly summarize what I know of the events leading up to her departure while Abigail's mother sobs and the Baker men start sweating and flexing their fists. Mr. Baker looks at his wife and then back to me. He sighs. "It seems there's a lot our daughter hasn't told us," he says.

"Well. I know she feels you have expectations for her, and that you seemed set in your feelings about her former lover."

"Not if he fucking laid a hand on my baby girl! Jesus Christ." He stands up and begins pacing. "Well why in the hell are you here? We need to find her."

Mae Baker cries again. "We owe her an apology!"

"I'd like to marry her," I add, which then immediately seems like the wrong thing to say. I thrust the flowers and chocolate into her mother's limp hands and hand her father the box of fresh eggs. "I mean eventually. Once we straighten all this out. I'm interested in working toward that eventuality with Abigail. If she'll have me back. Right now I'd just like to speak with her."

The Baker family exchanges glances until eventually, one of the brothers rises. "I'll go gas up the Suburban, Dad. Go find Abby."

36

Abigail

I get about two miles in my car before I lose my nerve. Of course, Mary Pat and some of the Acorns are at the gas station when I pull in to fuel up. In my haste to get the hell out of Oak Creek, I grabbed two armloads of clothes and tossed them in my back seat. Now Mary Pat peers in the window as we both wait for our tanks to fill. She drives a hybrid, so it doesn't take her long to wander over to me and ask if I'm headed to the dry cleaner.

"Something like that," I say, but she frowns and nudges Lamar and Javier.

"We were just saying this was the best Autumn Apple we've had in years. Isn't that right, Jav? We sold out of natural hangover remedy at the co-op."

The graying former economics professor nods, massaging his temples. "MP and I were planning a trip out to Lancaster today to stock up on some tinctures with the Amish Apothecary we know out that way."

I nod, thinking that sounds like a nice way to spend a lazy Sunday, actually, wondering what Hunter would have to say about herbal remedies in the age of modern medicine. Thinking about Hunter reminds me that he's probably having makeup sex with his bitchy wife by now to avoid having to pay her his entire life. I choke back a sob and force myself to smile at Mary Pat and the guys.

"I can't wait to see what you all bring back," I tell them. The pump clicks off and I squint toward the road out of Oak Creek. When I reach in my pocket to grab my credit card, I see my phone has a bunch of messages from Rose. She's got foreign dignitaries coming to town this week and I am really pleased with the research I did into foreign customs, the way I helped her craft talking points to emphasize how our Oak Creek strategic plan aligns with the Sri Lankan goals for raising well-rounded young citizens.

I'm not going to get to do this kind of work anywhere else. But I also know it'll kill me slowly to live beside Hunter and his wife, to hear them fucking through the thin walls of our duplex. Even if they move, I have no desire to run into him on campus, and Oak Creek is a small college.

I pay for my gas and wonder whether Rose would write me a reference to get a communications job somewhere else. Maybe back in Ohio…where my parents are furious with me for leaving and my ex boyfriend could go off the rails any time.

I decide to go to the bakery and make a plan. I indulge in a chocolate muffin. "Yes, Stu. One made with wheat flour. And butter. From cows."

The Oak Creek gossip tree doesn't take long to shake out some leaves, and Diana stomps in the door within a few bites of my muffin. "What's got you spooked, Baker?" She reaches for a chunk of muffin and I pull it back from her. "Oh, it's like that, is it? Stu!" She yells for the tired baker to bring her something decadent and I start to tell her about what happened with Heather earlier this morning.

"What a frigid witch," Diana says, chewing her croissant as Stu crosses his arms and looks pissed. "You know that's bullshit, right?"

I shake my head. "She said Hunter changed his mind about the divorce when he learned that Heather would get long-term patent royalties." I sniffle. "And she said he realized how much he needs her now that he's living without furniture, with fowl flapping around his living room."

Diana laughs. "Hunter never gave a shit about furniture. You know that by now, Abigail."

I shake my head harder. "The day I met him, he was upset that I had his headboard from his childhood bedroom."

She thinks about that. "I'm guessing that was more a 'my dad made that' thing than a nostalgic issue. Hunter only cares about tissue samples—"

"Exactly. He's just going to live with Heather rather than let her get control of his research and ideas." I start sobbing at the injustice of it all, wiping my nose in the wax paper that had been wrapped around my muffin.

Stu leans on the table and interjects. "Abigail, come on. You know Sara is a better lawyer than that. She's a fucking shark. Hunter gave Heather a payout this morning that won't even dip into his fancy protein powder funds."

"I don't know…"

"Look," Diana butts back in, "I know for a fact he was at Archer's office this morning signing papers, because he went to my parents' house to build a chicken coop afterward and my dad said he was actually whistling. Dad's back there now preparing a feast for the Sri Lankans. We can go ask him if you want?"

"Hunter was whistling?" I begin to wonder if Diana's words make sense. Surely if Hunter were being forced to choose a loveless marriage with his mean wife, he wouldn't be whistling about it.

I'm just so used to being denied the things that I find meaningful—the things I love. I let Diana guide me to the Crawford-Mitchell house, not quite wanting to cling to the hope that this could all be a misunderstanding calculated by a bitter woman.

As Diana and I walk through the back garden, we can smell heaven and hear chaos from inside the house. Daniel stands at the stove whisking madly, hollering to Rose in another room of the house.

I hear her dragging furniture, shouting about the Sri Lankan delegates and their preferred sleeping arrangements. "Would it kill you to give me more notice for these things?" He shouts. "Or better yet, house them at the Inn where Indigo is prepared for hospitality?"

"Daniel, I've told you a hundred times. When I succeed at these efforts, you get laid!"

Diana slams the door shut, interrupting her parents. She mimes gagging at me but pulls me further into the house. "Dad," she said. "Stop stirring the roux and tell Abigail everything you know."

"Oh, hello, dear," Rose says, walking into the room. "Hunter thinks you're in Ohio. He's gone there with his astronaut friend."

Archer, Diana, and I jog over to the high school when Archer gets a text that Hunter is on his way back. Archer confirms what Diana suggested, that Heather was trying to get Hunter back and didn't succeed, so she lied to me, hoping to get in one final dig before leaving Hunter's life for good.

My relief at hearing this is dwarfed by my sense of overwhelm that Hunter has gone to Ohio in search of me, gone to speak with my parents. What must they have thought of him, showing up out of the blue, with nobody to explain his brusque personality. "Oh, lord, Hunter interrupted football Sunday," I say, looking at Diana tearfully. "Wait. Why are we at the high school?"

Diana points to the sky, where I can see a helicopter approaching. "My brother called in a favor with the outer space dorks," she says, shouting above the noise. "These guys have fancy toys."

I slam my hands over my ears as the aircraft sets down on the lacrosse field. The pilot kills the engine and the blades slowly stop whirring. I squint through the cloud of dust that's been kicked up, to see Hunter in the co-pilot seat and…"Mom? Dad?"

My parents tumble out of the plane and come jogging over to me. My mom pulls me into her arms, sobbing, and my dad starts screaming that he is going to kill Jack just as soon as he lays eyes on him. This is certainly not the reception I anticipated from my parents, and I can't control my emotions as tears well up in my eyes. I let them fall as I sink into my mother's arms. From the corner of my eye I see Hunter, standing with his hands in his pockets, looking at me hopefully.

Once the blades of the helicopter finally slow, the pilot wags his eyebrows toward Diana. "You Crawdad's sister? I'm Digger. He tell you about me?"

"Don't waste your breath," Diana scoffs. "Come on, guys. You're attracting a crowd."

37

Hunter

Digger flies off with a promise to come visit the campus soon as a guest lecturer, and I escort Abigail and her parents back to the duplex. I'm not sure whether or not to follow them inside Abigail's half, as she seems distraught and leans on her parents.

Her father beckons me inside, though, and with everyone seated around her table, she tells them all about the events leading up to her departure from Greenwood. I see her father work his hands into fists as she summarizes the evolution of her relationship in the months leading up to her departure.

"But I also wasn't happy in my job there, Dad." Abigail collects herself and sits up a bit straighter. "I had to keep my degree a secret from you. And I was working toward your dream there. Not mine."

"Hell, Abby, we just wanted to make sure you were comfortable. You know, your mother and I had a long road to get to where we could afford name brand cereal. I never wanted that for you kids."

Abigail's mother squeezes her hand. "And I certainly didn't mean to pressure you into staying with a man who harms you, Abigail Baker! When I grew up, my only chance at being something was through your father. That's just how things were then. I only wanted to see you settled."

I begin to feel uncomfortable listening to the Bakers discuss their emotional journey, but then I hear my name on Abigail's lips. "Of course I appreciate the sacrifices you made to make sure I could go to college, Dad. But all that work is for nothing if I can't choose my own path once I get that opportunity. Fate led me here to Oak Creek," she says. "To Hunter, and Rose and this town that embraces me."

Abigail begins to tell them how she uses her skills to help my mother, how she helped organize the festival. Soon the three of them are crying, talking about a tour of the town square, and making plans to spend Thanksgiving here in Oak Creek. I'm still not sure how I fit into this, but I am desperate to speak with Abigail privately, to make sure she knows there is nothing left between me and Heather. That she, Abigail, is my priority.

"Mr. Baker, would you like to see my father's wood shop?" The three of them turn their heads toward me as I shift uncomfortably. "I just…know that a craftsman such as yourself would enjoy…"

"Sure, Crawford. Let's go."

Finally, with my father and Abigail's poring over the oak and maple boards in my father's shop, and my mother showing Abigail's all around the themed rooms she set up for the Sri Lankans, I have a few moments alone with Abigail.

She sits beside me on the garden bench, staring at the creek in silence.

"I thought you left town," I begin.

"Well," she says. "I started to. But then I really wanted to keep my job, damn it. So I came back and your sister told me the truth."

"Abigail," I say, taking her hand. "I was blinded by ambition. From the moment I finished college, I set my sights on the space agency and for years, nothing and nobody were important to me. Only my work." I rub my thumb across her knuckles, needing her to understand the emotions I don't know if I have words to communicate. "And I still feel driven by my work. That won't change. But meeting you has shown me that there is room in my life, in my heart, for...well, for love, Abigail."

"Love?"

I nod. "I would love to explore that with you, if you'll let me and join me. I am a free man now, thanks to Sara, and I promise you that I will never let my work distract me from my commitment to you again."

"I don't know if I'm ready for love, Hunter. I'm a mess."

This is not the response I expected. I feel a vise squeeze around my ribs as my heart stops beating. "But...are you ready for me?"

38

Abigail

My parents decide to stay in Oak Creek for a few days to see the town and learn more about the place I've told them I'm going to put down roots.

I get them checked into the Inn, and Indigo promises to take good care of them. Knowing Indigo, I suspect my parents might decide to just stay there forever. It's good to show them the people I've met, to let them see how the townspeople greet me warmly. I can tell my dad is comforted to see how nice my townhouse is and to know I can afford it on my own, with my salary from the job I love.

My oldest brother texted my mom to let her know Jack had an "accident" leaving the bar after the hockey game last night, and my dad grunts noncommittally at this news. He and Hunter make eye contact across the table at the coffee shop. My mother reads another message from my brother to her phone. "Oh dear. Jack somehow got his ear closed in his truck door. How does such a thing happen?"

My father clears his throat and leans forward. "Abigail, you picked a real nice town for yourself. I like how Rose appreciates you, honey."

I smile. This is strong praise from my father.

"But you know, you always have a home in Greenwood," he continues. "That's your home, baby girl. I'm just saying, if you want to come back, well…"

"Thanks, Dad," I pat his hand. "I will come back." Hunter gasps and I put my arm around his shoulder. "Just to *visit*. I'm happy here. I have a life here. There is still work I want to do here."

My parents sip their coffee and Hunter stares at me, his gaze as intent as ever. "Son," my father says to Hunter. "Is that friend of yours going to fly us back home or what? We're sort of stranded here, and it's almost game day…"

Hunter and I decide to drive my parents back to Ohio together. He and my brothers have made a plan to go retrieve my things from Jack's house, and Hunter promises me that I don't have to see him. I love how thoughtfully Hunter handles this situation, how he knows I feel uncomfortable at the thought of seeing Jack without my having to tell him.

In the days following the Heather fiasco, Hunter doubled down on his promise to be a good partner to me. He keeps a small notepad in his back pocket, and I see him writing things down, like "Abigail enjoys strawberries," or "remind Abigail about socks at bedtime —>cold feet on my calves."

I feel more seen, more carefully considered than I ever have in my life. I don't know what will happen in the future, if I'll feel content writing for Rose or if Oak Creek will call to me forever. But I know that this man by my side is here to support me, to appreciate me, and to bring me repeated, toe-curling orgasms.

Mom and I pack up the last of my things while Hunter and Dad check the oil in his car. She smiles out the window at the pair of them, Hunter gesturing at the synthetic oil and babbling about chemical residue, Dad listening skeptically. Hunter is nothing like any of us are used to, and I can tell my parents are ready and willing to learn to love his quirks.

Midway back from Ohio, we decide we don't feel like driving the entire way in one go, so Hunter checks us into a resort. "Hunter!" I gasp as he lifts me off the ground in the hotel. He tells me I can spend the entire next day in the spa if I want, "but first," he growls into my neck. "You have to spend the night on me."

People stare at us as he carries me bride-style to our room, but I forget to care about that as soon as he lowers me to the bed and starts peeling off my clothes. "I need you," I gasp, realizing how true this is as he sinks into me. His bare flesh against my wet heat feels like a homecoming, a joining of souls. I wrap my limbs around him and welcome Hunter deep inside, again and again, until we both forget what it meant to be apart.

39

Epilogue: Hunter

Digger agrees to pick Fletcher up at the airport on his way to Oak Creek. I am very uncomfortable at the idea of sharing my space with others again, and I truly wish my parents would stop bringing in foreign dignitaries to stay at their house. But Abigail insists it's not hospitable to make my friend and my brother stay at the Inn.

"Besides," she says in the morning on Christmas Eve, rubbing her bare, icy toes up my leg in bed. "They're on the other side of the duplex from us." Abigail insisted that I buy furniture for my half of the townhouse, outfitting the two bedrooms with a bed, a night stand, and a dresser so our guests could at least feel welcomed.

"Is Digger bringing Fletcher in a helicopter again?"

I shake my head and pull her closer. "He has some sort of high security vehicle from the agency."

Abigail sends me ahead to my parents' house to help prep the meal while she works on a round of revisions for her novel. After months of declining Mary Pat's book club, she finally agreed to join Enid's writing club instead and has eagerly spent her free time pecking away at a draft she won't let me read.

I open my parents' back door and kick the snow off my boots as I hang my coat on the peg. "Ah! There's my Wexler Prof," my mother coos, sliding up and wrapping her arms around me. Ever since Asa Wexler agreed to support my research at Oak Creek College, funding a full-time research professorship in the biology department, my mother has been giddily notifying alumni around the world. Donations have apparently been flowing in as people want to congratulate *her* on attracting such prestigious faculty for the college.

I'm ok being a cash cow for my mother. It keeps me here, close to Abigail, and gives me total freedom to work on my computations.

"When do you go back to the tin can," Diana asks, lining up her latest batch of winter ales in the ice bucket.

I smile, pulling her in for an uncharacteristic hug. "January," I tell her. "So I need you to watch over Abigail for me while I'm gone."

My sister snorts and shoves me away. "You better watch her yourself, asshole.

Use your video chat feature how 'bout it? I'm sure Digger can show you how it works."

Soon after, my brother Fletcher and Digger burst through the door. Fletcher carries a case of wine from Napa, where he's been on location most recently, and Digger brings a bag of chips he must have gotten at the gas station.

"Dr. M, Mr. C," he says. "Thanks for including me."

"Nonsense," my dad yells from the oven. "Hunter promised you'd bring a laser to slice the roast."

After dinner, when my family gathers in the living room to exchange gifts, I feel a sense of contentment I hadn't known was missing from my life four months ago. All of my siblings are together, which rarely happens, and my mom actually gets teary when Digger suggests a family photo by the tree. He pulls out a very expensive camera to take the shot, and when Dad tugs Abigail into the photo, I slip my arms around her shoulders and squeeze her close.

I still have to work to interpret others' emotions. I am still surprised at the ease with which Abigail can communicate nuanced ideas, and I've kept my promise to care for the chickens and, thus, *her* alongside my research. I don't know what force in the universe caused the confluence of our lives, but I am grateful.

Digger shows me the photo, where I am gazing down at Abigail as the rest of my family smiles into the camera. "I love you," I tell her, as my siblings bicker and demand a retake.

She grins and takes my hand in hers. "I love you, too."

Can't get enough of Oak Creek?
Jump right into Diana and Asa's book,
The Botanist and the Billionaire!

You can subscribe to my newsletter
so you never miss a new release:
laineydavis.com

Printed in Great Britain
by Amazon